A Candlelight Ecstasy Romance®

**HIS KISS WAS GENTLE, SOOTHING,
AND LOVING.
LOVING? LOREN PULLED BACK. SHE
COULDN'T OPEN HERSELF TO THIS
KIND OF HURT AGAIN.**

"I realize we can't just pick up where we left off six years ago, Loren. But could we try to catch up? Try to understand?" Reid's voice was almost a plea.

"Reid, we have both changed. We lead entirely different lives now. I'm not the same innocent young girl I was six years ago. And I won't let you manipulate me as you did then."

"Was it so bad?"

"The leaving was."

"All right. Let's give ourselves time." Resigned, he dropped his hands to his sides. "But, Loren, what was once between us, what we once shared, is still here. Don't fight it."

Loren stared, the events of the evening flashing before her like a fast-paced movie, ending with Reid picking up his jacket and walking out her door. Again. Then she was beside him.

"Don't go, Reid," Loren begged, knowing this was against all she stood for. "Please, don't go."

A CANDLELIGHT ECSTASY ROMANCE ®

ENDURING LOVE

Tate McKenna

A CANDLELIGHT ECSTASY ROMANCE ®

Published by
Dell Publishing Co., Inc.
1 Dag Hammarskjold Plaza
New York, New York 10017

Dell ® TM 681510, Dell Publishing Co., Inc.

Candlelight Ecstasy Romance®, 1,203,540, is a registered
trademark of Dell Publishing Co., Inc.,
New York, New York.

ISBN: 0-440-12379-8

Printed in the United States of America
First printing—September 1983

To Carol, Patsy, and Bev,
for the fun and fond memories.

To Our Readers:

We have been delighted with your enthusiastic response to Candlelight Ecstasy Romances®, and we thank you for the interest you have shown in this exciting series.

In the upcoming months we will continue to present the distinctive, sensuous love stories you have come to expect only from Ecstasy. We look forward to bringing you many more books from your favorite authors and also the very finest work from new authors of contemporary romantic fiction.

As always, we are striving to present the unique absorbing love stories that you enjoy most—books that are more than ordinary romance.

Your suggestions and comments are always welcome. Please write to us at the address below.

Sincerely,

The Editors
Candlelight Romances
1 Dag Hammarskjold Plaza
New York, New York 10017

PROLOGUE

He was following her again! She glanced stealthily over her shoulder and there he was! His dark head was bent, conspicuously angled toward the newspaper he held. But she knew he wasn't reading it. She faced the front of the subway car and felt his penetrating eyes on her! A chilling shiver ran down her spine and the bitter taste of fear rose in her throat.

Loren closed her eyes, trying to forget him, to relax. But who could forget him? And who could relax on the subway? She waggled loosely, like a disjointed doll, with the constant vibrations of the car against the rails, reminding herself this was the smoothest subway ride in the country. Or so they said. New, modern, sleek, efficient, convenient . . . nothing but the best transit system for the capital city.

Foggy Bottom . . . Arlington . . . National Airport . . . This exit was hers.

Loren's blue eyes flashed open. She gripped her briefcase with one hand and a seat arm with the other, bracing herself for the most exciting and beautiful city in the United States—Washington, D.C. *Her city.* Its pulse, its vibrance, its importance, thrilled her daily, making her ever grateful that she had grown up here. She was lucky enough to go to George Washington University, get a job on The Hill, and learn the ropes from the man who had known every knot and was responsible for looping many of them—her own father.

Loren merged with the crowd at the stop. *Did she catch a glimpse of him exiting?* She transferred to the bus for the short ride on George Washington Parkway. She sat nervously in the front seat, instinct impelling her to glance in the rearview mirror. *There he was,* his head towering above all the others. His appearance was distinctive and intrepid, bordering on handsome. Dark hair fell carelessly across his forehead and stylishly edged his collar at the neck. And those eyes! They were a deep mahogany color, almost black. And they seemed to drill right through you. Tall, lean, long-legged, he wore his suit clumsily . . . as though he would be shedding the coat and tie at any minute and begin to lope through the streets. He definitely did not have the three-piece-suit, tailor-made look of the Washington men she knew. Yet, he walked with a self-assured, broad stride, those long legs devouring his course impatiently. And those awful boots! *Cowboy boots,* for God's sake, with a suit! Actually they were the only items about him that looked natural.

The bus shook to a stop. Ah, Alexandria . . . *home.* Loren loved all the interesting sections of Washington. Georgetown . . . The Mall . . . The Hill . . . the Potomac . . . but Alexandria was her favorite. Old, quaint, traditional . . . a slower pace. She loved it. *Would he follow her? What would she do if he did?*

Loren left the bus and heard him dismount behind her. She knew the next move was hers. Allowing a few minutes for him to get closer, she whirled around to confront him. It would be wiser to face him now, while others were near and before reaching her town house. She couldn't let him know which tiny entrance was hers.

But he was gone! Out of sight! She scanned the narrow

cobblestone street, but he wasn't visible anywhere. Where could he have gone so quickly?

Heart pounding, Loren walked rapidly to her brick-edged doorway and inserted the key. At that moment a white Continental sped past, as much as a car could speed on a cobblestone street. She looked up in time to see that *he* was in the passenger seat, while another man drove. *There were two of them!* And now *they* knew where she lived! Oh, dear God! What a fool she had been! In her innocence, her ignorance, she had shown them exactly where to come! Feverishly she unlocked the door and hurried to the phone.

Oh, damn! She realized with a jab in the pit of her stomach that she hadn't checked the license plate! Mistake number two! With shaky fingers she dialed the phone.

Loren was assured, in an uninterested monotone, that police patrols on Prince Street would increase. Somehow she doubted it.

Aware that *they* knew where she lived, Loren spent a sleepless night, waiting in the still, cold hours of the early morning when *they* were most likely to break in.

But the anticipation was in vain.

CHAPTER ONE

*Breeze gentle as a poem . . . jewel in the sea . . . eternal
pulsings of the ocean . . . oaks of majesty and endurance
. . . sand like diamonds . . . love, like dreams . . . once is
never enough . . .*

She could hear the rushing, roaring thunder of the sea
as it crashed on the breakers, feel the warm wind in her
hair, see the brilliant glare of sand crystals in the sun,
smell the deep sea-green salty water as it sprayed her face.
Loren Randolph was bewitched, obviously whisked away
from the bitter-cold wind off Chesapeake Bay.

"Dreaming again, Loren?"

She jumped, then smiled sheepishly at the office recep-
tionist. "Sorry, Anne. I was just browsing through this
booklet that came across the congressman's desk. It's
about a resort island off the coast of South Carolina. Isn't
it beautiful?"

Anne craned her head to gaze over Loren's shoulder.
"Um-hum. Sure is. You'd think that since we work for
South Carolina's congressman, he'd invite us down there
sometime."

"Wouldn't that be nice? Well, perhaps he will. Spring
should be gorgeous there." Loren sighed. "But spring is
gorgeous here. I want to go somewhere *now.* I have the
winter blahs, I guess. Now, what were you saying before?"

The sleepless night was taking its toll, and she was extremely tired and slightly irritable.

Anne handed Loren a slip of paper. "There is just one more appointment. He insisted on seeing you."

"Why doesn't he just wait until next week and see the congressman if he wants a job?" Loren stole another glance at the travel booklet.

Anne shrugged. "He said he wanted to show you his credentials first. Probably wants to pave the way by talking to the congressman's aide initially. I told him you'd be glad to see him. Always the eager-to-please office staff of Congressman Neilson!"

Loren smiled wryly and waggled her head. "Oh, sure, sure. Did this man say anything else?"

"Just expressed an interest in wildlife management." Anne leaned forward and whispered huskily. "He sounded like some wildlife I'd like to manage! His voice was so . . . masculine!"

Loren smiled tightly at Anne's frivolity. Never had a man's voice affected her that way. And she continued. "I'm sure he sounded masculine for good reason. He's probably an unemployed DJ who wants to work in the country's most vibrant city. I'll check him out, Anne."

"Should I stay and . . . help?" Anne's eyebrows arched teasingly.

Loren smiled. "If he needs an appointment with the congressman, I'll be glad to schedule him when you're in the office."

"Are you sure you don't mind if I go home early today? Everyone else in the office has already gone."

"Of course I don't mind. I told you that earlier. This won't take very long. You run along. Will I see you at the ambassador's dinner tonight?"

Anne smiled as she gathered her purse and an armload

of notebooks. "Oh, yes. I have an appointment to get my hair done, so I do need to run. Thanks a lot, Loren."

Loren picked up her travel book and followed Anne to the front office. "I think I'll just wait for Mr., uh, Reed, out here at your desk."

Anne nodded. "Good idea. And Congressman Steiger's office down the hall is still open, so there are people close by. See you tonight, Loren." By the time the glass-encased door closed, Loren was already enthralled with her island resort book.

A shuffling noise preceded the rattling of the door and Loren realized her appointment had arrived. Reluctantly she tore her attention from the colorful page before her.

Broad, masculine shoulders blocked the doorway as dark, brooding eyes canvassed the room, settling on Loren, filling her with instant fear. *It was him!* The man who followed her home! The man who knew where she lived stood before her now, and she was all alone in the office! Her heart pounded wildly, then seemed to lodge in her throat as she tried to speak.

It came out hoarsely. "You!"

"Good observation." His smile was almost pleasant. "And you are twice as lovely up close."

She rose, her knees rubbery, intent on somehow getting past his figure in the doorway. "You followed me! Why?"

He entered the room, quickly covering the space between them. His boots resounded heavily in the empty room. "You interested me, and I just wanted to know where an aloof, attractive girl who worked on The Hill would live. And I'm impressed."

"Is the effort worth discussing with the police?" She was bluffing, but she hoped the anger in her voice was a threat.

"No harm done. I was just curious about you. Before

you call the cops, let me introduce myself." He extended his large brown hand. "Reid Mecena. My office is in the Dirksen Building. Don't you remember me?"

"Should I?" She was hesitant to reach out for that hand. Vaguely a flicker of recognition appeared. She had seen him before . . . somewhere . . . even before he followed her. But where?

"We've met. The first time was a few years ago at an inaugural party. The last was just last month when the White House hosted an awards ceremony for the Western Heritage Contribution winners."

"Oh." Slowly she grasped his still outstretched hand. "You're . . . you're Senator Mecena's son."

"Right." He grinned, revealing one incongruous dimple wedged in his left cheek. "And you're Jefferson Randolph's daughter, Loren. Jeff and my father were colleagues. We were sorry to hear of his death last year."

"Thank you." She tugged uncomfortably on her hand, still encased in his. "Perhaps I do remember you." She knew she had attended those functions, but racked her brain to recall this impressive man before her. Surely she wouldn't have dismissed him so casually.

"I haven't been able to get you out of my mind since we met, and I wanted to know you better."

She folded her arms defensively across her chest. "After the scare you gave me this week, I'll probably never get you out of my mind either! I don't appreciate your methods, Mr. Mecena. Do you know I called the police about you last night? You really frightened me."

"I suppose you could say I got your attention, but I'm sorry I scared you." He sat in the chair in front of her desk and balanced a manila folder on his knee. "I followed you once before out of curiosity. And you lost me. The next

15

time I was ready for that. You definitely are a challenge, you know."

"Why did you come in here today . . . and use a false name?" She still stood before him, glaring down at his seated figure.

He motioned to her. "Please, sit down, so we can talk."

In her own office he had the audacity to offer her a seat!

Then he continued, shrugging. "I wanted to talk to you. It's that simple. I wanted to see you, introduce myself, ask you out, without bringing my father's name before the entire office staff."

She continued to stand. "You would have gotten a better reception if you had mentioned him." She narrowed her blue eyes angrily. He had scared the hell out of her and now expected to apologize and proceed like old friends.

"As I said, I didn't want my father's name to be bandied about this office. I'm certainly not looking for a job, as I claimed. I'm in Washington to manage his office. I was looking specifically for you. No one else. And especially not Congressman Neilson!"

"Well, you have my undivided attention. What do you want?"

"When can we go out? Tonight?"

"I'm busy tonight. I have a date," she answered boldly.

"Tomorrow?"

"No, thank you, Mr. Mecena. I'm busy all weekend." She refused to encourage him. This man was intriguingly masculine, and he did have a nice voice, as Anne had predicted, but he was not for her. She must have decided this at their earlier meetings, which explained why she'd forgotten him.

"I heard you played hard-to-get. That's why I tried to find out as much about you as I could before our little encounter today. Don't forget, I know where you live."

"Is that a threat?" Damn him anyway!

He shrugged and answered with a slight grin. "Just a statement of fact, that's all. You won't get rid of me this easily. Why don't you sit down, Loren. Then we can talk without me craning my neck." He motioned her downward again.

This time she obliged, perching on the edge of the chair. "I think our conversation is finished."

"No, it isn't. Are you going to the ambassador's dinner tonight?"

She flashed her eyes briefly, then controlled her tone. "Maybe."

"Good. I'll see you there. Meanwhile, read my credentials. Anyone can tell you about me and my family. And I'm sure my father will vouch for me."

She stiffened. "I'm not interested in your credentials, nor in your father's high opinion of you!"

"That's too bad, because I'm very interested in you. And I need someone knowledgeable to show me around Washington."

"I'm not in the tour-guide business."

"Let's talk about it tonight."

"Don't bother trying to find me, Mr. Mecena. There will be approximately four hundred people dining tonight."

A wicked grin crossed his swarthy face. "But I have experience in tracking you, remember?"

Her blue eyes flashed. "How could I forget?"

Confidently he nodded. "I'll find you. It'll give us a chance to talk in the company of others. That's what's bothering you, isn't it?"

She leaned forward. "*You* are what's bothering me! Why don't you just leave me alone?"

He leaned forward too. "Because I'm in love with your

17

blue, blue eyes. They are the most fantastic eyes I've ever seen. Have you ever been to Texas in the spring, Loren, when the bluebonnets are in bloom?"

She shook her head.

His large hands spread expressively as he spoke in a low, mesmerizing tone. "Well, the bluebonnets carpet the hills around small towns like Navasota and Brenham with the most magnificent blue blossoms you've ever seen. And your eyes, Loren, remind me of those flowers. They are a vibrant color, with just a touch of violet. Like the bluebonnets. I wish you could see them."

Loren gulped, not daring to reveal that she could already visualize them from his vivid description. "I thought you were from Arizona."

"I am. But I've traveled quite a bit. And I swear there's not a prettier sight anywhere than those fields of bluebonnets in April . . . except your eyes."

She took a deep breath. "Flattery will not sway me, Mr. Mecena."

"Please, call me Reid. I'd like to show you those bluebonnets this spring, Loren."

"Don't plan on it." She couldn't seem to dissuade this persistent man.

"Oh, but I am. I think you would love it, Loren. This spring . . . don't forget. And tonight. I'll see you tonight, blue eyes." He made a notation in the folder, then closed it and handed it to her. "My dossier. Check me out. You'll find I'm respectable enough."

Angrily Loren stared after him, even after his square frame had disappeared through the door. He was unnerving, that man. *That man!* He was not at all the kind of man she was usually attracted to. His hair was too dark and his eyes too penetrating. But, then, no one caught her attention for long. The man was right in observing that she usually played hard-to-get. She was simply too busy to be hindered by the numerous males who pursued her in this town. She wasn't interested in these men who were too soon gone. Of course, no one had intrigued her like *this man. This Arizona man, Reid Mecena.*

She hoped fervently that she wouldn't see him tonight. Then he would know that her "date" for the evening was fifty-six-year-old Representative Steiger and two of his office staff. They all lived in Alexandria and generally went together to these dull functions. It gave them someone familiar to chat with.

Loren packed her briefcase with files she needed to read over the weekend. She would brief Congressman Neilson on Monday. There was always something to prepare for— which was what made her job so interesting. She picked up the folder left by that arrogant man. She certainly didn't want to leave it around for someone else to find. Curiously Loren let the folder fall open and glanced down the first page. Her eyes flew over the neatly typed information to the bold scrawling at the bottom of the page.

Make love in April in a field of bluebonnets with Loren, the girl with the bluebonnet-blue eyes!

"Damn!" Loren's mouth dropped open, and she snapped the folder shut and stuffed it into her briefcase. *The rude audacity of that man! First, he follows me home and scares the hell out of me! Then he gives a false name to the staff at my office and seeks me out personally! Now he hands me an official dossier where he has noted to make love to me—in a field of flowers in Texas yet! The nerve!*

The ambassador's dinner was crowded with the elegant-ly attired elite of Washington. Champagne and liquor were flowing freely under glittering chandeliers; the sound of affected laughter was everywhere.

"You wouldn't be trying to give me the slip tonight, would you?"

Loren's stomach gave a disparaging flip, for she knew that the masculine tones tingling her ears were from the very man she was trying to avoid! She wheeled around and gave a silent gasp, hoping fervently that her rapidly beating heart wasn't apparent through her low-cut gown. Musical strains from the full orchestra filled the background and, before she could respond to the man, Loren found herself swept into his sturdy arms and onto the dance floor.

"You know, of course, that you stand out in a crowd, even one of four hundred. Every man in the room is ogling you in that dress. The color exactly matches your eyes, and it exactly fits . . . everything!" He held her loosely, watching her face for a reaction to his bold statement.

Loren blushed all the way down to the creamy swells of her breasts, hating herself for not being able to control her emotions any better. Her frustration sputtered out in a small explosion. "I should have worn a black sack!"

"Ah, I would be able to spot you in anything, Loren. Those blue eyes can't be camouflaged!" His smile radiated through her, and she warmed under his gaze. There was also that single intriguing dimple in one creased cheek!

"Neither can your intentions, Mr. Mecena!" Loren prayed she was disguising the erratic beat of her heart as his dark eyes created havoc with her self-control. Even her skin tingled under his velvet gaze!

He pressed her closer, bringing her taut breasts in slight contact with his shirt. She could feel the warmth from his chest reaching out to her. There was a certain strength, an energy, that drew them together, and it frightened Loren.

20

She was trying very hard to dislike Reid Mecena, yet was pulled in his direction by invisible cords.

"I hope you'll soon feel familiar enough to call me Reid. I want to dance only with you, get to know you, Loren." His voice softly massaged the air. "That's all. Is that so bad?"

Loren took a reluctant breath, fearing he would hear its raggedness. "All right. One dance then." It was an unnecessary consent, since they were already dancing, but she felt better having agreed.

Reid loosened the tension apparent in his arms and shifted her closer. Her breasts swelled against his chest as she relaxed in his arms. They finished the dance quietly, allowing the magic between them to develop naturally.

For Loren, it was a reluctant effort. Her reason told her to hold back, be heedful, and proceed with caution. And yet her instincts wanted to throw caution to the wind. *Is that so bad?* His words rang in her head. No, she mused. It felt very nice, indeed, to be in his arms. Oh, yes, Loren could feel the magic!

When the dance ended they reluctantly drew apart, the cool space between them fanning heated emotions. Reid's dark eyes sought hers, questioning. For a brief moment Loren thought he felt the same magical attraction she did, then decided that was silly. It was a romantic fantasy, suddenly racing through her imagination. The band struck up again, this time a country tune.

"Since I don't see your date, Loren, shall we try another dance? "Blue Eyes Crying in the Rain" is one of my favorites, but you don't often hear it from an orchestra's strings."

His arms were around her easily, quickly. Or had she floated there eagerly? Later, when she recalled the eve-

21

ning's events, she wasn't sure. All she knew was that they spent a good deal of the night in each other's arms.

"I have an admission," Loren offered, wondering why she was so eager to confess.

"What?"

"I don't have a date tonight."

His breath was warm on her ear. "I know."

"You do?" She drew back to look up at him.

"I did a little surveillance earlier this evening. You don't think I would risk encountering the outraged escort of such a gorgeous lady, do you?"

"After the way you behaved this last week, I wasn't sure what you would risk encountering!" she answered smartly.

"You are definitely worth the risk, Loren," he murmured against her ear. The velvety softness of his breath sent chills down her spine, and she longed to sink closer to him, to press against his hard chest. Of course, she did not. After all, they barely knew each other. Perhaps tonight would be a time for remedying that.

"I've never met a man so bold." *Or one who made me feel this way.*

"I'm captivated by you, Loren Randolph. I've never seen eyes quite the color of yours. They're enchanting . . . and so are you." His voice was a hoarse whisper and wrapped around her as securely as his arms.

"You're a silver-tongued devil." She laughed.

"Who's intrigued with you, Loren."

"A secret admirer?"

He nuzzled her ear ever so faintly. "You'll find that I don't work in secret. Nor do I admire in secret. I want you to know exactly where I stand."

"I . . . I think I do, Reid." His name felt strange on her tongue, even though she felt so familiar in his arms. So

22

right. "Reid . . ." she repeated it again, just to hear the sound.

When the dance ended he asked, "Could I persuade you to abandon your seat with old fuddy-duddy Steiger and join me for dinner, Loren?"

She laughed spontaneously at his fitting description of Representative Steiger. "With an offer like that, how could I refuse?"

"Good. I have a table reserved for us in the back. If we're lucky, maybe no one will sit with us. I want you all to myself. There are a lot of things I'd like to know about you, Loren Randolph." His hand steered her to the table.

"There are many things I'd like to know about you, too, Reid. The first is, How on earth did you manage without your boots tonight?" She halted beside her chair and noted his shiny black shoes with a wry smile.

Reid's lips curled into a good-natured grin. "This is my monkey suit, reserved especially for these dressy Washington affairs. Believe me, young lady, if you weren't among the guests here tonight, I wouldn't be here either."

Loren eased gracefully into the chair and waited until he sat next to her at the large round table set for six. She, too, privately hoped no one joined them. "I see your father is here tonight, Reid. In fact, Senator Mecena is at the honored guests' table."

"I manage only my father's office and campaigns. I do not attend every function he does. I stopped being infatuated with the Beautiful People long ago."

"Why, to see you tonight, Reid, I thought you were one of them," Loren teased. She couldn't help admiring the way the tuxedo fit his lean form.

Reid nodded for the waiter to bring them wine. "Because my father has been in politics for as long as I can remember, I'm accustomed to these events. I can shoot the bull with any crowd, and I know which fork to use when there are more than one. But, I'll admit, I prefer to be in my jeans and boots."

"I can tell."

"Is it that obvious?"

"Oh, it's not that you look out of place. It's just that you have a casual, western look, like that jacket is in your way and you might be shedding it any minute."

He laughed aloud. "It has crossed my mind, but I won't embarrass you, Loren." He waited until the waiter had poured their wine, then lifted the crystal glass to toast Loren. "To a lovely lady."

"Thank you," she murmured. Their eyes met over the wineglasses, mesmerized by the silent magic weaving between them.

Finally, reluctantly, Loren initiated the conversation. "Tell me, what was it like to grow up in a political family in Arizona?"

He shrugged. "Just about like it was for you, I guess. Only my father was gone from Arizona quite a bit. When he was home, life was chaotic, but fun. There were always people in and around our house. Some were guests, others there for business. Something always going on. When we didn't have a full house, we had invitations to just about everything that came to town. We always had tickets to the circus, ice show, ballgames, things that kids love. I finally outgrew the freebies and left the social events to my father. Sometimes I went along to the political speeches to hand out brochures or simply to read the crowds. Later Dad and I discussed their reactions, moods, that sort of thing."

Loren laughed delightedly. "Yes! I've done those things for my father too!" They had more in common than she thought. Somehow it was a small assurance.

They were joined by two other couples at the table, and Loren tried to mask her disappointment. She would have to share Reid. Still, she felt close to him tonight. Just the two of them, attuned only to each other, alone in a crowd of four hundred. During the course of dinner Reid enchanted them all with tales of living in Arizona. Loren listened, almost charmed, certainly intrigued. There was nothing to relate this engaging man to the menacing one who had followed her. By the end of dinner it didn't matter that he had made brash claims about making love to her. In fact, it was hard to believe Reid was that same arrogant man. Maybe she just didn't want to believe it.

Afterward they danced again. Loren floated in Reid's arms, her blue eyes meeting his in an unspoken agreement.

"How about coffee? Someplace private?"

She agreed, never doubting the prudence of going with him. "I know a wonderful little Bohemian spot in Georgetown."

"Great! I've been wanting to get you alone all night."

"We have been—" The words slipped out before she could stop them.

"You know, you're right." He held her, even though the music had stopped. Their eyes locked, and Loren knew he felt the magic, too, even if neither understood.

"There is so much more I want to know about you, Loren."

"There is so much I want to say . . ."

By the end of the evening, Loren Randolph trusted *that Arizona man* . . . and more. She was fascinated by him.

They rode around the beautifully lit tidal basin before crossing the bridge into Arlington County and home. Reid drove with precision to the cobblestone street and stopped in front of her narrow-doored brick town house. Why shouldn't he? He had been past the place often enough.

25

Loren turned her face upward, not feeling the chilling wind off the Potomac that whipped around them. The touch of his lips on hers filled her with an unquenched desire, unlike any she had ever experienced.

"I'll see you tomorrow," he promised.

"You'd better wear your grubbies if you do. Saturday is gardening day in Alexandria. It's an old tradition."

"In the middle of winter?" His breath was frosty. "What in the world are you doing? Planting bluebonnets?"

She blushed at the mention of his first promise. "Hardly! This is mostly clean-up time, getting ready for spring flowers. A few crocuses have already poked up through the snow."

"I'll help you tomorrow on one condition," he proposed.

Loren looked up questioningly into his dark, shadowed face.

"That you'll go out to dinner with me tomorrow night. Someplace special . . . just the two of us."

Loren caught her breath. Even though she hardly knew him, she wanted to be with him. Perhaps dinner would be okay . . . just dinner.

"That would be nice."

The next day Reid appeared in well-worn jeans and an old sweater. They spent the warmest part of the day working in the tiny garden that nestled between Loren's tall brick town house and the identical one to the rear. They raked and bagged the winter debris of leaves and sticks; Loren mapped out a new flower bed; Reid turned the soil for her. When the wind began to whip down between the brick buildings and the afternoon sun was blocked from the small garden, they sat in Loren's cozy yellow kitchen, drinking hot spiced tea and nibbling anise cookies.

It was almost dark when Reid returned to take her out for the evening. Loren opened the door to a man who was clean-shaven, his dark hair brushed back neatly, his navy, pinstripe suit framing his broad shoulders precisely. God! He was handsome! Loren gasped at the sight of him. She had never considered him handsome before—appealing, intriguing, darkly masculine—but never handsome. Well, he was still rugged and square-jawed, with lines running beside each cheek. She thought of that hidden dimple. Her eyes traveled down his length.

His voice was impatient. "Do I pass inspection, or must I stand out here and freeze?"

"No boots!" Loren laughed, moving aside for him to enter. "You didn't wear your boots!"

"Of course not!" He closed the door behind him and cupped her face with both hands, kissing her nose lightly. "I don't want to embarrass my lovely Washington lady by appearing to be a boorish clod in cowboy boots! But I still feel naked without them!"

She laughed, giddy with the closeness of him. "Oh! Your hands are cold!"

"Sorry. See what a boorish clod I am? Think I can fake it tonight?" He moved his hands to her arms, which were covered with puffed long sleeves of old lace and eyelet that allowed small patches of pinkish skin to show through. "Loren, you're beautiful. This dress . . . it's gorgeous, just like you."

"Do you like it?" she breathed, wishing he would take his hands off her so she could think straight.

He dropped his hands to his sides and stepped back, assessing her appearance. "It's unusual, old-fashioned. And you look lovely in it."

Slightly unnerved by his overwhelming presence and lavish compliments, Loren fingered the old lace. "This

27

dress belonged to my grandmother. It's been in our family for years."

"My God," he grinned, revealing the dimple. "I'm escorting an heirloom tonight! Ready to go?"

She nodded and grabbed an intricately crocheted shawl. As his hands draped it across her shoulders, he asked, "Another treasure from your grandmother?"

"No," she answered as they glided out into the frosty night. "My elderly neighbor gave it to me. The one who made the anise cookies. She's originally from Germany and has fantastic skills that most modern women, including myself, never take time to master. Isn't it beautiful?"

"Ummm." He nodded, encircling her shoulders with his arm.

"She crochets these to sell, and I sometimes help her by getting orders from my friends. Her income is quite limited, and I try to help her whenever I can."

"Sounds like the two of you complement each other." He opened the heavy car door.

"I suppose we do," she agreed as she slid into the plush blue interior of the white Continental.

Reid covered the distance around the car quickly and sat close beside her. "I like to think we complement each other, too, Loren. You're elegant and lovely and smart. I'm rough and unpolished—"

She interrupted. "And bright and very interesting and . . ." His face was unnervingly close to hers.

"And attracted to you, Loren Randolph." His lips, warm and sweet, caressed hers gently, lingering to savor her honeyed taste.

In the brief moment of that tranquil kiss, Loren forgot everything around her. She was drawn to Reid's ardent warmth, the frigid air suddenly ceasing to chill. She immediately dismissed her personal policy to remain aloof to

28

the men she dated, especially those from out-of-town. She disregarded the fears this man had engendered just yesterday when he faced her alone in the empty office. Loren knew only that she was physically, emotionally, wildly, attracted to this man who kissed her so gently, yet thoroughly. And she wanted this feeling to last forever.

"We'd better go," he breathed, moving reluctantly away from her willing lips. "Before we freeze."

"I'm not cold," she murmured before she thought.

His hand slipped under her thick tawny hair. "I know . . . oh, God, Loren, don't tempt me so!" He moved as if to kiss her again, then turned abruptly, started the car, and wheeled out onto the bumpy, cobblestone street.

Minutes later Reid pulled to a stop before a looming four-story brick-and-stone warehouse. "How about seafood?"

"Love it!" She smiled happily. "And the Seaport Inn is one of my favorite places. The view over the Potomac is gorgeous."

"I don't know about the Potomac, but the view across the table will be gorgeous," he said as they ambled along a two-hundred-year-old brick sidewalk.

"Do you like seafood too?" She gazed up expectantly.

"No, but I knew you did." He steered her to the narrow wooden stairs that creaked as they stepped up together.

She paused at the top. "How do you know so much about me?"

"I made it my business to find out. I told you, Loren Randolph, I'm terribly attracted to you." He smiled and touched her nose with his index finger, and Loren had the feeling—perhaps the private wish—that if they hadn't been in such a public place, he would have kissed her again.

The ancient heavily wooded shadowed interior probably enhanced the romantic mood of the evening. But they didn't notice. Loren and Reid were indifferent to the mysterious and dark waters of the Potomac, the symmetrical designs of city lights glittering across the river, an occasional foghorn. They had eyes and ears only for each other.

She leaned toward him as the waiter removed their soup bowls. "How could you waste it, Reid?"

His dark eyes flickered at her. "I, and the children in Arizona, would starve before we'd eat those floating things in our soup!"

Loren feigned shock. "Oyster stew? Why, that's an East Coast mainstay!"

"Maybe for you. But not this unrefined oaf." He paused while the waiter served their dinner. "How can a lovely *señorita* like yourself eat . . . that?"

Her blue eyes widened. "Don't you like lobster either?"

He plunged his knife into the juicy steak before him. "Only if it's disguised. Definitely not staring at me with those little beady eyes and its pincers poised!"

Thus they spent the evening teasing, cajoling, and learning that in many ways they were not very much alike at all. But it simply endeared Reid to Loren all the more. She adored every minute. Reid was funny, interesting, and extremely western. And she loved being with him. They lingered over coffee, not saying very much. Just enjoying . . .

So it was no surprise to either of them when, at her front door, she asked him in . . . and he accepted. In the bluish shadows cast by the colored shade of the old Tiffany lamp Loren and Reid stood close, entranced with each other. Slowly his hands eased up her lacy sleeves, cupping her face, tilting it upward to his. Eagerly Loren complied, for she wanted to feel his kiss again, absorb his masculine heat, touch his beguiling face, search for that hidden dimple.

Loren sank against Reid, and his kiss was as bewitching as she remembered, only stronger, more powerful, more wonderful. His gentle caress changed to a forceful, desire-filled entreaty as Reid's hands slid around her shoulders and ranged her back, molding her ever closer to his lean-muscled form. The softness of his lips was gone as he engulfed her mouth with his. Lost in his virile demands, Loren felt the first tentative tickling of his tongue over her sensitive lips. His probing was a trial, seeking surety of her response. To his delight, Loren opened to meet his quest, accepting the rhythmic force he offered.

Although young, and somewhat innocent, Loren was certainly aware of her own feminine responses to Reid's sensuous masculinity. And she wasn't ashamed to let him know. She met his probing with her own warm tongue, matching his motions with bold actions of her own.

Instinctively his hands clasped her buttocks, thrusting her hips to his, revealing his male strength and passion. The sensation was too much for Loren and, although she had responded quite eagerly until now, the raw male form propelled against her so boldly was more than she could bear.

"Oh, Reid! No!" she breathed, her blue eyes wide and full of a million expressions.

His hands edged up her back, caressing, stroking, persuading her in a nonthreatening way. Reid wanted her desperately tonight and knew by her responses that she wanted him too. However, he sensed her inexperience. One minute she was a wild temptress eliciting his excitment, the next she was a wide-eyed lamb, trusting him, yet not trusting.

"Loren . . . Loren, you're so tempting . . . so beautiful," he groaned.

In response, Loren's hands slid inside his jacket to stroke his firm chest, then around unmoving ribs to clutch the taut muscles of his back. "Reid, you are the most exciting man I've ever met. I can't believe what's happening to me . . ." she breathed. His hand slid around to cup her breasts, sending new, uninhibited sensations coursing through her.

"Loren, *mi querida,* you know you want me. Don't deny it. Say yes . . . I must have you," he pleaded hoarsely, his thumb amusing her nipple.

Say yes? Suddenly Loren was hesitant. "I . . . I don't know . . . it's too soon, Reid. It's crazy!"

"Don't be scared of me, Loren. I won't hurt you. I couldn't. You're too special . . . too precious."

"I'm not scared of you, Reid." Her voice was a whisper, for inside herself, Loren knew what she was leading him to . . . agreeing to. And she couldn't believe her own sounds.

Reid had never shifted away from her, and Loren could still feel the swell of his masculinity against her. "Loren, darling . . ." His voice was ragged. "I can make it special for you. For both of us. You are everything I need in a woman—beautiful, smart, responsive to me and only me . . ."

She tried to move away. "And . . . inexperienced . . ."

He nibbled at her ear. "At least you're honest about it."

"I want our relationship to be honest. And I don't want it to end after tonight."

"Oh, God, no," he murmured against her neck, assured that he would have her tonight.

"Do you promise? Reid . . ." She was serious.

He looked deep into her blue eyes and answered fervently, "I promise, Loren. It won't end . . . ever. I love you."

His words whirled in her head. "This is insane, Reid. I feel like I'm in a daze."

He reached down and picked her up in his strong arms and walked slowly up the stairs to her bedroom. "We're in a daze together, Loren. And that's what makes this attraction between us so very special. It was immediate. We're drawn together, Loren. We can't deny it, so why try to fight it? Let's enjoy it . . . and each other."

Her bedroom was dark, but outlines of furniture were visible as their eyes became accustomed to the dimness. He stood her in the middle of the room, awkwardly fumbling with the million unwieldy pearl buttons that divided the front of her antique dress. When they were finally undone, he peeled the fabric back from her bodice and over her shoulders as if he were unwrapping a package. She wore a lacy pink-and-beige-silk teddy, and his male fingers clutched at it, scooting it down over her curves.

Loren stood before him unashamed and proud of her body. Her breasts were two creamy mounds, naturally well-formed and uplifted, peaked with strawberry tips, firm and ready for the picking. Her hips flared ever so slightly from her slim waist. They blended into straight, compact thighs. It was those thighs he touched, unable to keep his hands off her any longer. He scanned her entire body length with his hands, aware of the ripple of desire that shivered over her. As his hands cupped her enticing breasts, she reached for him.

"Now you," she ordered in a hoarse whisper.

Eager to comply, to have her, Reid dropped his jacket beside her heirloom dress. While his hands tore at the stubbornly knotted tie, Loren began on the row of shirt buttons. By the time she had finished, he had unzipped his slacks, which also joined the growing heap of clothes at their feet. Another quick movement and he stood before her completely nude, aroused, and impatient to take her in his arms.

Almost shyly she touched him, running curious hands over his rocklike muscles, combing through the dark mat of masculine hair that curled on his chest and trailed to his flat belly. When he could stand no more, he wrapped her in his arms, burying his face against her soft breasts.

He lowered her gently to the bed, murmuring promises of love forever. His skill at lovemaking convinced Loren that Reid was no novice. The thought reassured her, and she relinquished herself to his care. She believed his passionate promises because she wanted to, and trusted his erotic leadership because it worked. She found her tightly coiled body relaxing . . . and enjoying.

"My sweet, beautiful Loren," he murmured as his hands stroked and excited her, teaching her. His lips encircled each rosy tip, finally bringing her urgently to arch against him, begging for fulfillment.

Their coming together was as swift and passion-filled as their brief, magnetic acquaintance had been. The flash of lightning that consumed them both feverishly brought forth a sudden feminine cry. Then silence. And, in the darkness, low masculine rumblings.

Reid comforted her, repeating gentle words of love. As he cuddled her against his chest, he felt pangs of remorse. After all, she had given herself to him completely and trustingly.

But Loren refused to allow him his somber, dispirited mood. She had been fulfilled as a woman, by the man she loved. And hadn't he said he loved her too? She ran her fingernails over his chest. "Did you know that a sea captain once owned this house?"

34

He nuzzled her neck. "Wonder if he and his wife made love in this room."

She laughed. "I'm sure somebody did! Whether it was the captain . . . who knows?"

"What do you mean?"

"Well, the Hessian soldiers who were taken prisoner were forced to lay these brick sidewalks we have. And one of them escaped and hid out in the attic of this house while the captain was off to war. When the soldier was discovered by the captain's wife, she just couldn't turn him in. Eventually they became caught in the captive/captor syndrome. And she gave in to his wicked ways. . . ."

"Wicked? The poor fellow was starved for affection and a woman's gentle touch!" His laughter rumbled in the darkness.

"Like this?" Loren giggled and ran her hand tauntingly over him. "I always wondered how they communicated, though, if she spoke only English and he spoke only German."

Reid's leg draped over hers. "Oh, that's easy. They spoke the universal language of hands!"

"Hands?" She laughed, her voice tinkling in the quiet.

"Um-hum, like this . . . and this . . . and this. Soon she got his message. And they were conversing like crazy!"

"Brilliant!" she mused, then cuddled against him like a kitten. "I think they fell madly in love, and when the war was over, they escaped together!"

"What a romantic you are!" His hands caressed her tenderly.

She nibbled lightly on his neck. "Incurable!"

"Then you like my universal language?"

"Of course," she murmured low. "But I always thought the universal language was love!"

35

"It is. I think it is, *mi amor,* and we have a tradition of love to follow. Hold me close. . . ."

They conversed in their own special language, and, as Reid promised, their love didn't end that night. Nor in a week or a month. It continued long enough for them to make love in the Texas bluebonnets, delight in Washington's cherry blossoms, walk along the sandy beach off the coast of South Carolina, and embrace the spectacular autumn at Valley Forge.

Yet, when the winter winds whipped across the Potomac, they nipped mercilessly at Loren's solitary figure.

CHAPTER TWO

Loren gazed around the ancient room filled with heavy wooden furniture as they made their way to a table for two near a window. She could never enter the Seaport Inn without thinking of *him*. They had spent many happy hours here. . . .

"Ah, this is perfect. Excellent view of the Potomac, isn't it, darling?" He helped her with her chair. "See what you've missed by refusing to come here?"

"Yes, it's lovely, Mark." How could she tell him that whenever she returned to this place the ominous feelings were so strong, so overwhelmingly awful, she could almost reach out and touch them. And tonight was no exception. There was an eerie, almost tangible feeling in the air. Loren shivered and looked out over the Potomac River to the array of lights from Washington.

"Cold, darling? Would you like Chablis? Loren?"

She nodded absently. "Chablis sounds fine."

They toasted their impending wedding and exchanged small talk, but mostly spent the time gazing out the window to admire the view. A foghorn penetrated the silence between them, and Loren jerked her head up, startled, the sound creating a memory. They sipped the oyster stew, and Loren smiled to herself as she pushed "those things" around in the bowl, remembering *his* dislike of seafood and the subsequent teasing. *Oh, dear God, I've got to stop this!* She gulped her wine and immediately a white-coated waiter appeared to refill her glass. She turned her gaze across the room, waiting.

And there . . . there he was! Their eyes locked for a second that seemed like a lifetime before she turned away. Her thoughts were wild and jumbled as her blood pumped furiously through her veins. *I must be seeing things! I thought it was him! But, it just couldn't be! Not after all this time. Six years of trying to forget. And now I think I see him again. How much wine did I have? Only one glass? Why do I feel so crazy?*

With a shaky hand she lifted the glass to her lips and drank boldly. Then her eyes, drawn like a magnet, sought that same table where he sat with two other men. His profile was in her line of vision now, and she examined the man carefully, curiously, oh, God . . . afraid. This man was different, but somehow the same. Dark, unruly hair, penetrating, almost-black eyes, his squared shoulders were crammed into a suede jacket, and *he looked as if he would shed that coat at any minute!* The man's appearance was very rugged. And those boots. *The same godawful scuffy cowboy boots!* The mustache was what made his face look different. The man turned and watched her again, his eyes catching hers. And she knew. *She knew!* It was all Loren could do to keep from spilling her wine. With jerky motions she set it on the table and scooted her chair back.

"Excuse me, please, Mark."

"Certainly, darling. Are you all right? You look a bit pale."

She nodded and tried to smile. "I'll be right back." Loren carefully avoided the dark stare from across the room as she made her way quickly to the ladies' room.

38

Once inside, she slumped against the wall, taking deep, gulping breaths to try and calm her heaving stomach.

A patron was drying her hands. "Are you all right?"

Loren nodded mutely, and the woman left.

In the quiet, sanitarily fragrant room Loren began to laugh. Hysterically, wildly, incoherently, even to herself, until the laughter dissolved into tears that flowed down both cheeks. She grabbed a paper towel and wet it, dabbing at the smeared mascara under her eyes. She gaped at her reflection. Pale-cheeked, red-eyed, stricken, she looked terrible. Taking her time, Loren repaired her makeup, hoping the redness around her eyes would soon go away.

Could that man actually be Reid? *Reid.* But he was, and she knew it. What was he doing here, so far away from Arizona? And why would he come here, to this particular restaurant, of all the fabulous places to dine in D.C.? Why, for that matter, did she and Mark come here tonight? She wished a thousand times over she had never agreed to it!

Taking a deep breath, Loren smoothed her skirt and straightened her blazer. She still wore her working clothes, the tailored suit, so chic, yet businesslike. She could face Mark now.

Stepping out into the dark hallway that led to the ladies' room, Loren was momentarily blinded in the dimmed light. A hand shot out and grasped her wrist, pulling her against a solid male body. Alarmed, she prepared to scream. But something prevented it.

His voice . . . "Loren, Loren—"

She gazed up, very close to the man's face. *Reid Mecena!*

Loren gasped audibly, then, with more composure than she could ever dream possible, muttered, "Excuse me, please." She tried to move away from him.

39

But his hand did not loosen its grip. "Loren! Loren, thank God, it's you! I wasn't sure for a minute."

Frantically she looked into his familiar eyes, the eyes of an intimate stranger. "Please, leave me alone!" she begged.

Anguish instantly shot across his face. "I can't! Now that I know it's really you, Loren, I must talk to you."

"No! Please, Reid, don't do this to me!"

His voice was tight. "Loren, I don't understand. Do you mean that you don't want to see me? Don't you have any feelings? I must know how you are . . . what you're doing!"

Loren finally jerked her arm free from his firm grasp. "For all you care, I could be dead by now! Will you please move so I can pass?"

"I want to see you again, Loren. Do you still live on Prince?"

She turned her head away, trying not to give him any information . . . trying not to care.

His voice was a low rumble, so familiar yet so distant. "Do you still live in the sea captain's house where the Hessian soldier made love to the captain's wife? The house where *we* made love, Loren? Surely you haven't forgotten."

Unable to avoid his gaze, Loren turned back to Reid's sad eyes. "I haven't forgotten," she whispered hoarsely.

"Can I see you there?"

For some unknown, uncontrollable reason, she nodded. Her head moved of its own accord, imperceptibly, yet positively. No words were spoken between them for long seconds as each was caught in the magic of the attraction that still existed, after all the years that had passed. In her mind Loren knew she shouldn't do this . . . knew she was betraying herself. *Again.* But she couldn't help it. She had to see him again too. Just this once.

Reid's hand touched her shoulder, and the warmth

40

flooded through her, electrifying her senses. "I don't want to disturb your evening any more than I already have, so please return to your table. I won't interrupt and ask for an introduction. I'm afraid I might punch the man in the nose."

She smiled for the first time since seeing him, responding to his once-familiar banter.

"I have to see you alone, Loren. When can I come?"

She shrugged, her eyes saying a million things.

"Tonight?"

Loren nodded. "Give me a little time." *Why? Why was she doing this to herself?*

"See you later." His promise was a whisper as Loren slipped away from his overwhelming presence. She stumbled back to the table where Mark sat, disturbed because she had been gone so long.

"I almost sent the waitress in to see if you were all right."

"Sorry, Mark. I—I ran into an old . . . friend."

"How nice," he remarked indifferently.

Loren took a sip of her wine, hoping it would calm her jagged nerves. But her hand shook so that she had to steady it on the table.

Mark motioned toward her plate. "Try your crab imperiale before it gets cold, dear."

Loren attempted to eat, but the creamy fare knotted in her stomach with every bite. So she pushed it idly around on her plate until Mark had finished his dinner. Every time she glanced up and across the room, Reid's eyes were on her. Totally unnerved by his presence, as well as his promise to see her later, Loren claimed that she didn't feel well and was ready to leave.

Miffed by her strange behavior and abrupt termination of their very elegant dinner, Mark whisked her home in a matter of minutes. He crammed the key into the lock and stood aside for her to enter before him.

But Loren placed her hand on his arm and said, "Don't come in with me tonight, Mark. I don't feel very . . . sociable."

"Loren, are you sick?" Irritation was obvious in his tone.

She shook her head. "It's just a headache. I have a lot on my mind. It's . . . it's a tough case next week. I need to work on it this weekend."

His hazel eyes snapped at her. "You and those goddamn liberated women's cases! There's always one that has you over a barrel. When are you going to get smart and work for some decent clients?"

Instantly Loren bristled. "These *are* decent clients! Just because they don't have the money yours do—"

"Oh, Loren, you know what I mean. These women seem to leave themselves open for the problems they have. They keep going back to the same goddamn man who beat them up month after month. Or return to the jackass who chased every skirt he saw. What do they expect?"

"Expect? Like anyone else, Mark, they expect love!"

"Oh, hell! They just keep going back—and they deserve what they get!"

Loren was shaking with anger. "There's no excuse for what some of my clients have endured!"

His hands grasped her forearms. "I'm not offering excuses. I'm trying to get you to see how futile your job is. These women ask for trouble, and you spend all your time bailing them out—for a pittance!"

"In some of these cases I'm all they have! Their last resort!" Loren sighed and lowered her voice. "Look, Mark, I'm not going to stand here on my doorstep, defending my job. Nor will I argue women's rights tonight."

42

Ruefully he backed down. "I'm sorry, darling. You know I'm as strong an advocate of women's rights as anyone. It's just that I see you working too hard on these causes. And I wanted you all to myself this weekend. I'm disappointed."

She touched his cheek. "I'm sorry, Mark. Not tonight. Please—"

He shrugged. "Okay, Loren. I won't press. But I'll see you tomorrow." He kissed her cold, unresponsive lips, murmuring, "Goodnight, my love."

She waved as his car rumbled away over the cobblestones.

Loren walked slowly into her small home, lit only by the varicolored Tiffany lamp. She stared numbly, not bothering to turn on another light. The house was cool, but she didn't even think to turn up the thermostat. She just sat on the sofa, hugging the heavy granny-square afghan around her. She felt excited and scared, sensitive and paralyzed, all at once.

She squeezed her eyes shut, trying to block out his new image, his old memory. But the bold, dark vision loomed in her mind, and Loren saw his profile close and felt his breath on her face and heard his low mumbling of her name. Reid looked older, more mature, with a little gray mingled with the dark hair at his temples. Well, he must be about thirty-four or -five now. The lines beside his cheeks were deeper etched, and she wondered about the dimple that hid in his left cheek. He was still lean and western and wore his jacket as though he were on the verge of discarding it. Oh, God, he was handsome! And now his mustache was a newer, more stylish complement that added character to his already interesting face.

A car traveled the rough cobblestone street, passing by her house. What if he had forgotten where she lived?

43

Where they had made love? No, that wouldn't happen! What if . . . he didn't come? After all this mental anguish, what if he didn't show up? Just like six years ago, when he left and didn't return. Sinking back into the depths of the sofa, her head lolling back, Loren resigned herself to the idea. She could make it without him. After all, she had managed adequately alone for years. But, so far, she hadn't seen him again . . . hadn't looked into those deep, dark eyes. Loren thought she couldn't stand the idea of Reid being in Washington and not seeing her. There was no telling how many times he had previously been in Washington and not bothered to look her up though.

Another car rapidly turned the corner and pulled immediately to a practiced stop in front of her brick walk. The driver obviously knew exactly where to stop. There were three hard, familiar knocks on the door.

Taking a deep, ragged sigh, Loren gathered the afghan around her chilled shoulders. Then she was there, opening the door, facing him.

She looked so lovely, so vulnerable, so achingly proud. Her tawny hair, shorter than before, barely reached her shoulders as it curled over the familiar afghan that she was clutching. Her eyes were the same, more intense perhaps, as when they had laughingly made love in the field of bluebonnets. Her lips and neck and arms were tense— begging for his touch—yet holding back from him. He wanted to caress her, to hold her, to crush her to him! But, did he dare?

There was a lightness in his tone. "Aren't you going to ask me in?"

Loren smiled faintly, then stepped back to admit him, once again, to her home . . . her life.

As Reid stepped into her home he was suddenly, powerfully, overwhelmed with the sights and smells around him.

44

He was back! *Déjà vu!* This was where he belonged! He knew he couldn't leave her ever . . . *ever* again. He gazed at her upturned face and immediately Loren was propelled into his strong arms. His lips devoured her ravenously while a low moan escaped from deep inside him. Finally, after an eternity of time and memories, he released her, murmuring, "Loren, oh, my God, Loren, how I've missed you."

Loren stumbled back, obviously shaken by his actions and words. She hadn't expected . . . or had she? Maybe she had moved into his arms of her own accord! "Please, Reid, don't—"

He ran his hand raggedly over his face, then placed it on the wall above her head. "I'm sorry, Loren. I didn't mean to offend you. I just couldn't resist you. I don't know how I stayed away so long."

"I don't know either." Her voice was a hoarse whisper and she turned away from his closeness. She curled into the corner of the sofa, letting the afghan fall from her shoulders. The air was suddenly warmer.

Reid stuffed his hands into his pockets and glanced with satisfaction around the once-familiar room. He began to walk around, stopping occasionally to touch a lamp or wall hanging. Some were things they had purchased together while rummaging in old antique shops or browsing through art galleries. But he didn't mention that. He didn't have to. They both knew. He gazed at Loren finally, with great contentment written on his face. "Some things never change. It's just as I remembered it."

"But people do," she responded sadly.

"Yes," he admitted. "And people keep living, doing what they have to do. Only you look . . . the same. Perhaps lovelier. The years have been good to you, Loren."

She smiled bitterly, wondering why she wasn't gray and

45

bent with all the sadness she'd held inside during that time. Did she dare tell him how hard the years—and life without him—had been? How much she hurt? "I just did what was necessary to keep going all these years. I'm sure they took their toll."

He smiled slightly and white teeth flashed against his tanned face. "It doesn't show. You're lovely."

Poignantly she answered, "The scars are all inside."

"Loren, please—" he implored, hands palm out. "It was tough on me too."

"Well, what did you expect, Reid? Did you think I would fall into your arms the minute you walked in the door? Did you honestly believe that our relationship could pick up where it left off—six years ago? No way!"

He swallowed hard, knowing she was right . . . and terribly hurt. As if he couldn't stand the intensity of the moment, he changed the subject. "It's cool in here. I'll get the heat." He walked confidently to the hall and adjusted the thermostat. "How about a cup of hot tea? Then we can talk. I think there's a world of things to be said."

She shrugged neutrally. She had thought a lot about this moment over the last six years, and now he wanted to delay it. "Help yourself. Or should I say, 'Make yourself at home'?"

His dark, devilish eyes cast her a menacing glance, but he refused to answer her caustic statement. Instead he proceeded to the kitchen, opening the cabinet where he knew she stored the tea. "Is Constant Comment okay?"

Loren nodded silently and remained on the sofa, feet curled comfortably under her, watching Reid work around the kitchen. She found herself enjoying the sight of him puttering in the yellow kitchen, as he had done so many times in the past. Oh, God, it had been a long time. Six years! Six heartbroken, hard-working, life-building

46

years for her. And now, how dare he step back into her life? How could he think he had that right? And how in the world could she allow him in? Was she absolutely crazy? Things were going too well in her life to disrupt it now. There would be only one reason that would merit the discordance a relationship with Reid would surely create. Only one. *If their love was strong enough.* But, Loren wondered, could she relent to love?

She focused again on Reid moving about the tiny, well-organized kitchen. It was no surprise that he had shed his jacket, draping it casually over a chair. As his muscular arms and shoulders rippled with his movements, she remembered those arms around her. His chest strained tautly against the beige shirt, and she recalled times when that chest had pressed lovingly against her own. His dark hair fell in casual disregard across his forehead, and Loren could see strands of gray not previously there. The lines in his forehead and along his cheeks were more deeply etched, indicating that the years had taken their toll of him. Perhaps his life had been difficult . . . but, no. She wouldn't provide excuses for him.

Reid reached for the cups, the dainty china that was always dwarfed by his large ranch-style hands. Once, as a joke, she had bought him a mug, one to fit his hands. His western hands were made for mugs—something large enough for him to grasp. The mug was a tacky thing, with a roadrunner imprinted on its side. But Reid had laughed that marvelous low laugh he had, and always insisted on using it.

His sudden low laughter jarred Loren back to the present. He had found it! It had been tucked away, hidden from her sight, but saved, nonetheless. *Saved for tonight,* as if she had known all along that he would return. *And leave again.* A chill passed through her at the thought.

47

With a lingering smile on his face Reid set the tray carefully on the table before her. The smile was broad this time and revealed the incongruous dimple in his left cheek. Loren returned his smile and accepted the delicate china cup and saucer he offered. In his typical masculine way he grabbed the mug—his mug—and sat beside her. She caught his leathery, manly scent, which reminded her of all outdoors. She had forgotten that. Loren smiled because she still loved that smell . . . still loved him.

There was a smile in his voice. "You saved it. My mug was well hidden, but still there."

She shrugged. "It belongs."

"Like everything else around here?"

Her heart reached out to him. *Like you,* she thought. "I suppose so."

He set the mug down and turned to her. "I've missed you, Loren . . ." He moved closer, overwhelming her with his fragrance. It had been so long since she had been close enough to smell his marvelous masculinity, feel his warm, inviting lips on hers, know his immediate response to her being there.

His kiss was gentle this time, soothing and loving. *Loving?* But Loren pulled back. She had to. She couldn't—wouldn't—open herself to his kind of hurt again.

She drew in a shaky breath. "Please, don't, Reid . . ."

He shifted away from her, feeling her reluctance to his presence and yet confused by her varied reactions. Sighing, Reid gulped the hot, spicy brew from his mug. "It's been a long time since I've had this flavor tea, Loren."

"About six years?" She sipped delicately, feeling better as the warmth spread throughout her insides. "Why? Won't your wife prepare it for you?"

His dark eyes cut into her. "Tea wasn't my former wife's type of drink. Scotch was more to her liking."

Loren raised her eyebrows. "Former wife? I see we have a lot of catching up to do."

He answered honestly. "Yes, we do. I just hope you'll give me a chance to explain. Give us a chance again, Loren. We shared too much happiness to let time and bitterness drive us apart."

"I thought by inviting you here tonight I was being quite open-minded. The bitterness? It was six years in accumulating, Reid. One night of explanation won't erase that."

"I realize we can't just pick up where we left off six years ago, Loren. But could we try to catch up? Try to understand?" His voice was almost a plea.

She smiled longingly. "We can try." She reached for his face, just to touch it, caress it, run her fingers along the lines and touch the grayness in his hair. "I . . . I've missed you, too, Reid. And you know something funny? At first I wasn't sure it was you in the restaurant tonight either. It was almost like a dream, my imagination. And yet you're still the same. These lines are deeper, a few gray hairs that weren't here before. And this mustache . . ." She touched it curiously. "I like it. Gives you a distinguished, mysterious appearance." Her hand fell away, and suddenly she felt shy with him.

Reid's tone was soft and serious. "Loren, I want you to know that through it all I have never forgotten you or the love we shared. You have always been in my memory. Always. And when I saw you tonight, I knew I had to talk to you . . . to hold you again. Just once more. Can you understand that, Loren?"

She nodded, muttering thickly, "Of course."

He kissed her forehead. "And you are the same as in my memory."

She sighed. "I won't deny that what we shared at one

time was special and wonderful, Reid. But we have both changed. We lead entirely different lives now."

"I know, but we're still the same people," he insisted.

Loren shook her head stubbornly. "I—I'm not the same innocent young girl I was six years ago. This year I'll be twenty-nine. And I won't let you manipulate me as you did then."

His voice was rough. "Was it so bad, Loren? I thought you enjoyed it too."

"The leaving was."

"That was a mistake. I sensed it then; I know it now. I was wrong to leave you, but my life just seemed to cave in around me after that and . . ."

"Your father? How is he? We heard about his stroke."

Reid grimaced. "It's been very difficult for a man who was once so active. Now he's confined to a wheelchair, and that's tough. But he's doing fairly well, considering."

"I'm sorry to hear that. I can't imagine him inactive."

Reid shook his head. "You probably wouldn't recognize him. He's lost weight and is very bitter. Dealing with him is difficult."

"How do you handle him?"

"Oh, I have help at the ranch," Reid admitted gratefully. "I could never get along without Lupe and Manuel and Raul, plus we've hired a therapist who comes weekly. They help me run the ranch and take care of my father."

"Do you mean you're not a senator from Arizona yet?" she teased.

He chuckled, embarrassed that she should touch on the very timely subject. "No, not yet. That's a few years down the road, I suppose. Right now I just manage the ranch's business."

"A gentleman rancher? How nice." Somehow that didn't sound like work to Loren. Certainly it wasn't nine to five, dress for success, and meeting the daily pressures of "a job."

Reid's hands became expressive. "It's the life-style I really love, Loren. I have freedom, open spaces, and enough to keep me busy and in tune to people and what's going on in my state."

"Your state? How quaint!" She chuckled.

Reid laughed with her. "I guess that does sound possessive, doesn't it? I see you're still spirited, Loren. I like that. And you haven't lost the ability to excite me like no other woman."

"Like no other?" There was acid in her tone. "What kind of fool do you think I am, Reid? You were married! Someone excited you then!"

His answer to her was low-toned. "I was married for two miserable years. It was sort of a land acquisition marriage, with two powerful ranch families joining. It had been arranged for years. And I thought it might work. After all, she was a native Arizonan and could understand the life-style. Believe me, Loren, there was never any love —never anything like what you and I shared here in Washington that year."

She gave him a doubtful look. "Please—don't!"

"It's true, Loren. What we shared was very special— always will be. What about you? Are you—" The obvious question was avoided as he lifted her left hand, cradling it, running his fingers around the sparkling, sizable rock that graced her third finger. "What's this?"

"I'm engaged," she answered quietly.

"To the man I saw you with tonight?"

She nodded silently.

His voice was tight. "Do you love him?" Then, after a heavy silence, "Do you sleep with him?"

She sat the cup and saucer on the table with a clatter,

51

and stood. Anger shook her voice. "I don't think it's any of your business!"

He was instantly beside her, his hand on her wrist, as if feeling her wildly racing pulse. "I have to know! Is it any good with him? As good as we had it?"

"Damn you, Reid Mecena! What the hell are you trying to do to me? Did you sleep with your wife? Was it 'good'?" Loren was dangerously close to tears. "Have you slept with a hundred women since me? Would you tell me the truth?"

His voice was low and strained and she could hear his ragged breathing close to her. "I'll tell you the truth. It was never as good as with you, Loren." His hands grasped her forearms and he shook her slightly. "Never, do you understand? I could never get you out of my mind! I tried! Oh, God, did I try!" His mouth was set in a thin line as he pulled her closer. "Tell me, Loren, was it as good? Was it ever as good?"

Loren's blue eyes filled with tears as she looked up at him, knowing she was once again opening her heart, her life, for love's pain. Her voice was low and hoarse. "No, Reid. It was never as good as our loving. Never."

"Oh, Loren, how I've longed to hear you say that! Oh, God, don't marry him! I want you so . . ." His voice was lost in the muffled groan that escaped his throat as their lips met.

His kiss was fierce as he pulled her powerfully to him, his actions vowing never to let her go. And she submitted to his strength, his clamoring for her. At that moment Loren never wanted to be out of his arms and free again. Being free would mean being without Reid. And, dear God, she couldn't stand that again.

Finally, breathlessly, he raised his head, raining kisses over her eyelids, and cheeks, and earlobes, and neck. Her arms clung to his shoulders as if she would never let him go, and, indeed this night, she didn't intend to.

"Oh, Loren, I want you so." He buried his face against her neck as his hands searched her back and shoulders, slipping under the tailored jacket.

Painfully she tore away. "Please, Reid, give me time."

"Time for what?"

"I . . . I don't know," she gasped. "This has all happened so fast. I just . . ."

Resigned, he dropped his hands to his sides. "All right. Let's give ourselves time. But, Loren, what was once between us, what we once shared, is still here. You know it as well as I do. Don't fight it." He ambled into the kitchen and picked up his jacket, hooking it over his shoulder.

Loren stared, the events of the evening flashing before her like a fast-paced movie, ending with Reid walking out her door. Again.

Oh, no!

She was beside him, her fingers digging acutely into his arm. "Don't go, Reid," Loren begged, knowing this was against all she stood for. "Please, don't go."

CHAPTER THREE

The piercing, insistent jangling of the phone roused Loren, and she reached for it in a half stupor.

"Um-hum," she mumbled. The bed was cozy and so very comfortable that she hated to move. But the phone wouldn't hush.

The voice was clear and strong. "Loren, darling! How are you this morning?"

"Hum?" With a start Loren recognized Mark's eager voice. She stole a guilty glance at the tousle-haired form of the man in bed beside her. "I—I'm still in bed, Mark." At least it was the truth!

"Sorry I woke you, darling. But I wanted to see how you're feeling. I'm heading out to the regatta today and wondered if you wanted to go."

The bronze-toned man beside her began to stir, sliding one wiry-haired masculine leg over hers.

Loren's mind wandered, then she remembered she was supposed to be sick. Well, she'd better sound like it! Her voice was somewhat shrill at first. "Oh, no! I mean . . . Oh, I couldn't possibly go sailing today. My stomach is still too squeamish."

A large, firm hand snaked across her stomach, then spread lower on her anatomy, curiously probing her navel. The distracting touch sent shivers down both of her legs.

Mark's voice came anxiously over the phone. "You're still sick? Loren, darling, do you need to call a doctor?"

The warm hand cupped her breast, teasing the soft, relaxed tip.

Breathless, she urged, "No doctor! I, uh . . . it's just a touch of the flu. I just need some rest."

"Can I bring you something, darling? Chicken soup? Seven-Up?"

"Ohhh . . ." That naughty nipple puckered tightly, and Loren found concentration difficult. "Please . . . don't!" Marvelous pressure was applied equally to each soft mound, and Loren's voice came out in spurts. "Mark, don't come over here. You . . . might catch it! Whatever I've got . . ."

A low, masculine voice rumbled in her ear, "He'll catch it, all right! Guaranteed!"

Mark sounded reluctant. "Well, if you're sure . . ."

Relief—or insane passion—swelled her voice. "Oh, I'm sure, Mark. I just need time to recuperate. All I want to do today is rest." She smothered a giggle as the dark mustache tickled her ear.

The masculine voice rasped again in her ear. "Just rest? Ah, nuts!"

"Well, darling, sorry you're feeling so bad and can't go with me today. I'll call tonight and see you tomorrow for sure," Mark finished confidently.

The phone clicked before Loren had a chance to say she might be "sick" tomorrow too. Deception was not her style, and she found that she wasn't comfortable with it . . . for a moment. She cradled the receiver and turned, smiling, to the captivating man who lay beside her. Mark was immediately forgotten.

Reid's features in repose were so familiar, yet strange; so customary, yet rare. The jet-black hair fell casually over

55

his forehead, excessive lashes hid those devilish eyes, the untempered mustache framed his marvelous lips so that only the bottom of his top lip was visible. And where was that elusive dimple? Her finger explored the tanned cheek, then edged his lower lip. White teeth nibbled at the soft pads on the tips of her fingers. Warm lips encased them completely with a sensuous sucking motion. His hand riveted possessively around her bare waist, pulling her half under his aroused, male contour.

"Was that your lover on the phone?" he growled.

Instantly Loren stiffened. "He's not my lover! We . . . we're engaged. Mark is—"

Reid interrupted. "—a fool for believing you! And for leaving you alone with me for even a minute! I should have followed my baser instincts and punched him in the nose last night! How rude of him to disturb us this morning!" His ebony eyes opened, and Loren felt herself sinking helplessly into their enchanting depths . . . into Reid's spell.

She struggled for some degree of decorum, wrestling with her own conscience. Mention of Mark reminded her sharply of what she had done. "Oh, Reid. I shouldn't have. I lied to Mark. I told him I was sick."

His heavy leg hooked over both of hers while his skillful hand traveled impartially to each ivory breast. "And you did that very well, *mi amor*. I say he deserves it for disturbing us!" He nuzzled her ear, his sharp tongue tantalizing the sensitive shell.

"Reid—"

"What's wrong, *querida*? Got the guilts?"

"Reid, you don't understand . . ." she implored as her arms clasped automatically around his neck. "We can't continue this . . . this way." Her taut breasts arched ach-

56

ingly against his hairy chest, and she moaned slightly as outrageous sensations coursed through her body.

"*Dios mío,* you're so right!" he groaned. His enthusiastic smile revealed the roguish dimple somewhere beyond the dark mustache. "And I have the only solution to our particular problem." He caressed her rib cage, slender waist, flat belly, all the way to the soft, downy tuft. His knee insinuated itself between her thighs, and her femininity was unequivocally responding to his mastery once again.

"Reid . . . oh, oh, Reid . . ." Loren buried her face against his corded neck, kissing and nicking at the skin.

"Oh, God, woman! You're enough to drive a man crazy!"

Her hands dug into his shoulders fiercely. "Look . . . who's talking . . . about crazy . . ." she gasped. "Reid, please."

"Oh, no, you don't! I want to enjoy you to the fullest, my beautiful blue-eyes!" He flipped the cover off them, and with one hand at her waist and the other snugly driving her crazy, pulled Loren atop his nude length. "I want to see all of you, Loren. To know if my memory serves me right. Damn, I've missed you! Missed this!"

She laughed giddily at his boldness, and her own wild abandon. She had missed him too. Missed his brazen admissions, his ardent lovemaking. Loren wriggled erotically over him, struggling to balance herself aboard his muscular form.

"Sit up, Loren," he groaned. "I want to see all of you. Here, this way . . ."

Before she knew what was happening, she sat astride Reid's well-knit frame, laughing, enjoying, responding to his touch again. *Again! No more dreams!*

"Ah, *perfección!* Loren, *mi querida,* I've missed this!"

His fingers lightly traced her already sensitive breasts, tantalizing her with his electric approach to the identical arches before him. Then, with an exclamation of pleasure, he cupped and lifted the convex curves, enhancing their size. He buried a kiss deep in the valley between them.

His male admiration of her soft feminine body sent torrents of desire shooting through her, and Loren had difficulty sitting still. She placed her hands on his ribs, bracing herself anxiously. "Reid—"

"Easy . . . easy . . . not yet," he admonished. His thumbs and forefingers gently twisted the dusky rose tips, and they pouted immediately. His guttural chuckle was full of undisguised masculine satisfaction. "I love to see that! To see you respond to me, and only—" He halted and didn't finish the obvious statement. His dark-fire eyes sought hers, the passion obvious, the unasked question smoldering behind tight lips.

As if in answer, Loren leaned back against Reid's propped-up legs. Her smile was one of extreme pleasure and untapped desire. Should she tell him that he was the only one who excited her with his touch . . . *the only one, ever*? "Reid, I love you to touch me like that. You make me feel so . . . so wanted."

"Ah, *mi amor*, you *are* wanted. So much, you'll never know . . ."

His hands traveled down her silken skin, tantalizing and manipulating her soft femininity, exciting and thrilling her. Reid loved her as she had not been loved for six years. Loren closed her eyes in ecstasy, glowing in the shockwaves of passion that fired her veins.

Time became endless as hot currents charged her limbs, engulfing Loren's senses beyond control. Reid commanded and dominated her body, and she followed his authority and mastery eagerly and willingly. It had always been this way. He, and only he, knew how to gauge her responses and charge her to the height of her yearning. Reid's dark image had even invaded her dreams, holding and exciting her, just like this. And she would awake in a heat to find herself alone.

Maybe this was a dream too. She had to know, to wake up before . . . oh, God! "Reid . . . Reid . . ." She reached for him, scraping her fingernails over his crisp yet velvety chest hairs, grasping the tiny, hard buttons she found there. In her half-drugged state she squeezed sharply. Was he real . . . or still a dream?

"Ow!" Reid's very real, loud yelp penetrated Loren's erotic dreams. "Devil-woman! What the hell!"

Loren jolted awake, shocked at his loud expulsion disturbing her dreamlike mood. Then she was embarrassed by her own roughness. "Oh-oh! Sorry! I . . . wanted to see if you were real," she muttered inanely. "I've dreamed about you for so long, Reid. I guess I can't believe you're real."

"Come here, devil-woman," he chuckled, pulling her over him.

Eagerly Loren pressed her taut nipples against his hard chest, weaving erotically to enhance the sensations of her smooth skin gliding on his. The aroused pebbly tips grated over his irregular torso, so muscular and hard beneath her silken softness. She relished his touch, and dug her fingers into his shoulders to brace herself.

His abundant hands caressed her back, trailing downward to stroke the curve of her buttocks. A wild hunger, unsatisfied for years, intensified Loren's passion. She bent her head to tease his button-hard nipples with her tongue, then allowed the moist taunting to thread its way over his most sensitive places.

"Loren—" The sound was rather strident from his

59

throat. He buried his hands in her tawny hair that lay tousled against his tanned skin. "Oh, God—"

It was exactly what she had been seeking. His response to her was vigorous and impelling. This was no dream! Reid was real! "Touch me, Reid! I want you to . . ." she rasped against his ear.

His hands obeyed her commands, teasing and stroking until she was fully ready for him. Then, with a low groan, he gathered her in his arms, rolling her under him. His breath was hot and uneven. "Oh, God, I want you! Loren, *mi amor,* see if I'm real now! This is no dream—" He slid between her legs, pausing maddeningly to brace his arms on either side of her.

In that frenzied moment Loren reached for him, arching impatiently to satiate her burning hunger. "Reid, Reid—" His name sizzled in the morning as his lips covered hers. He filled her with his throbbing passion and they were one again, lost from the real world for timeless, ecstasy-filled minutes, longing never to return.

Their bodies came together with the same furor as their kisses, all-consuming and fierce. His tongue eased past her open, willing lips to plunder her honeyed depths.

Reid's heated force was met with Loren's eager yearning, the two as one in their blazing frenzy. A volcano of fire spiraled within her as Loren felt his hands dig under her hips, pressing them even closer. The waves of Loren's desire rose higher and higher, mounting with the deep thrusting rhythm that encompassed them both. An eternity of ecstasy . . . never-ending fervor . . . the feverish crest of passion . . . an explosion of precise timing as they reached a climax together . . . and Loren knew she was Reid's forever. Their love had endured separation and time. She would always love him. Always be his to love.

They returned to the real, sunlit world, drenched in the

sweet moisture of love. Reid shifted, brushing her tumbled hair back, lightly kissing her eyelids. Loving words rumbled from deep within his chest.

"Reid, oh, Reid," Loren moaned when she could finally catch her breath. "It's so good to have you back. So good . . ." Once again, sensual pleasure and complete satisfaction were a part of her existence. There was no denying that need, but it was one only Reid could fill.

When Reid's passion was spent and he slumped against her, Loren collapsed in a tirade of tears. They were silent streams, tears of emotional joy. Of relief. But when they fell damp against Reid's shoulder, he raised his head, alarmed.

"Loren, *preciosa,* what's wrong? Did I hurt you?" He kissed her entire face tenderly as he placed his arms on either side of her, bracing himself over her.

Loren shook her head as Reid's lips continued to kiss, to lick, the tears away. She smiled up at him, the remaining mist glistening in her blue eyes. "No, of course not. I'm just so happy to have you back with me. The only time you hurt me was when you left."

The grim reminder sent a shudder through him. "Ah, Loren, *mi amor,* my beautiful blue-eyes. Never again will I leave you."

"Never? Oh, Reid, never?" Her eyes opened wide.

He kissed her again, lightly caressing her smooth skin. "I would have to be a fool, wouldn't I?"

She smiled wryly. "It happened before. . . ."

"Okay, I was a fool once. But not twice. This . . . you are too wonderful. Our love will conquer whatever the future holds." And his lips sealed his promise with tender passion.

Loren listened and believed him, wanting with all her heart for his words to be true.

* * *

After sharing the shower they dressed quietly, each lost in personal thoughts. Loren slipped a violet caftan over her head, ran a quick comb through her hair, and applied a dab of lip gloss. Glowing with contentment, she crossed the room as Reid's low voice sang a disjointed medley of Neil Diamond tunes. She paused by the door, her hand gripping the wooden facing. Remembrances flooded her. How many times had they lain together, arms and legs entwined, listening to the dynamic Diamond sounds? Or argued good-naturedly about which of his albums was best. They had even taped certain favorites to take along on a picnic to Valley Forge one time. *Oh, Reid, that was so long ago!* And yet he still sang their love songs. How could he? Unless, in his mind, things were unchanged. *Was it possible?*

Loren swallowed the heavy lump rising in her throat and padded down the steep, curved stairs, deep in remembrance of their once wonderful love. Could it be that way again? By the time Reid joined her in the kitchen, coffee was brewed, and she was thawing a frozen coffeecake in the microwave.

"What a wonderful morning!" he crowed. "Wow! You're absolutely beautiful in that color, Loren. Almost matches your eyes. Course, I like you in nothing!" His hands embraced her from behind, and he planted a succulent kiss on her nape.

"Morning," she purred. "Coffee?"

"Sure. I love to follow my morning exercise with hot coffee," he teased, kissing her earlobe from behind.

"Reid," she protested, turning with the intention of pushing him away. But her arms snaked around his neck, and she found herself resting against him. "Always? Do crambling. I don't even know anybody in the Department of the Interior anymore."

Loren cut herself another square of the cake and smiled ly. "But I do."

"What?"

"Reid, I've lived here all my life. I've seen them come and go. And I know who's in. In fact, we are attending a ner given by the Deputy Chief of the Interior tomorrow night. I could see that you're included. It would give you a chance to meet some influential people at the Interi." She stuffed another bite of cake into her mouth.

"Hey, Loren, that would be great! Would you do that for me?"

She reached across the table to caress his face. "I'd be happy to do anything you need, Reid. You know that. Anyway"—she smiled teasingly—"it wouldn't be a boring evening if you went."

Reid stood and refilled their coffee cups. "You know we could make a pretty good team, Loren. With your connections, maybe I'll get you to work for Arizona's water yet."

"Reid, I'd do anything to help you, and if that means helping Arizona, that's fine too. I'll bet if I put my mind to it, I could come up with several others who might be willing to listen. You'll need all the help you can get when the time comes for voting."

He drank his coffee with renewed interest. "You're fantastic, do you know that, Loren? What have you been doing with yourself these past years? Are you still working on The Hill?"

Doing? she thought acridly. *Crying a lot.* Her tone was considerably lighter than her thoughts. "Oh, I've been busy. I don't go downtown any more than I have to. I continued as Dick Neilson's aide for another year, then started law school."

you *always* follow your morning workout with coffee?" She grabbed his ears threateningly.

But he laughed and exclaimed, *"Mi amor,* I haven't had a morning workout like that in six years! Not since you, Loren, and you know it." He kissed her sweet, smiling lips securely, convincingly, and she wanted to believe him.

Abruptly she tore her lips away from his. "Ow! Prickly beast this morning, aren't you?"

"That's the way it is with us hairy men. Twenty-four hours without shaving and I have the beginnings of a beard. You don't happen to have a razor stashed away, do you?"

She grinned and scraped the stubble of his dark beard. Funny, she hadn't noticed his prickly chin earlier. Loren combed her fingers gently over the marvelous sable mustache. "How about some Nair?"

He made a face. "No, thanks. You'll just have to endure this stubble awhile longer." He kissed her again, and she experienced the soft sensations of his mustache above her lips in contrast with the sharp pricks of his overnight growth of beard. But she didn't mind at all. It just added to the proof that he was not a dream!

"Reid," she finally mumbled, pushing gently against his firm chest. "Our coffee's getting cold."

He shifted obligingly, and Loren turned to retrieve the cup. She dumped the cold liquid into the sink and fixed him another, this time steaming. "Black?"

He nodded. "You remembered."

She grinned. "It wasn't very complicated."

Reid walked around the cozy yellow kitchen with his coffee. "Things are still the same around here. No, the microwave's new." He bent to gaze out the window into the precise, symmetrical garden. "New tree. What kind is it?"

"Cherry. The blossoms were beautiful this spring." Loren relaxed at the small round table, pleasantly content to have him poking around her home again.

"Who—" He halted, not looking at her, not finishing his partly verbalized thought.

"Who helped me plant it?" Loren asked with a wry smile. "Mark." It was an impulsive statement. Perhaps that wasn't what he was thinking at all. Maybe he didn't really care who helped her. Why in hell had she even said it? She could have bitten her tongue.

Reid pressed his lips together and acknowledged the fact, continuing to amble around the sunny room. What did he expect? She was only human . . . and feminine . . . and sexy. He appeared cool, but inside he burned. It wasn't the tree-planting, or engagement rings, or quiet dinners that bothered him. It was the thought of Mark's hands inevitably on her that drove him crazy. Of the shadows of them alone in the dark. Of the image of them entwined in that bed . . . *their bed* . . . upstairs together. Suddenly his fist crashed onto the counter, scattering the cups they had left the night before.

Loren jumped.

Reid appeared as startled over his action as she was. His dark, smoldering eyes caught hers in a fierce gaze. Then, just as quickly, it softened. "Sorry, Loren. I . . . don't think I broke them. It's just that I was . . . oh, hell . . . it's cracked." He turned back to straighten the cups. One was broken.

"Reid?"

"It's broken. This one's cracked." He sounded as sorrowful as if it had been a major catastrophe.

She jumped up. "Not your mug!" Surely not his tacky mug with the roadrunner! Somehow it was significant!

He handed her the fragile handle of po dainty one. The mug's sturdy, still the sa

Relief flooded her face, and Loren be "Thank goodness! I like that stupid mug. G same."

And she was in his arms, pressing her fervently. They held each other for a long clinging to memories that were not quite l wanted them to be forgotten. Perhaps, the hope . . .

When they finally parted they were serious a Quietly they prepared breakfast together. Lor table and divided the scrambled eggs on small pl rated with yellow flowers. "What are you doing ington, Reid? I don't think I took the time to a smiled impishly, knowing full well why she hadn the time.

Reid cut them both a chunk of cinnamon-and topped coffeecake, then sat opposite her. "I'm lobbying. You know Arizona's ever-present need for water. There's to be a new bill before Congress this fall. I'm fighting that battle again."

In a half-starved manner, Loren quickly polished eggs. Then, alternating bites of cake and sips of coff commented. "Interesting. I guess you would be the one to lobby for Arizonans."

He shrugged, amazed at her rapidly diminishir "I was the natural choice. Because of the years n and I have spent in Washington, I'm supposed contacts here. And, with the ranch, I certain] personal interest in the water needs of southern

She nodded. "Sounds logical."

"Trouble is, half the connections I had six ye retired or have been voted out of office by no

"Law school, eh? Get tired of informing old Neilson on everything that was happening in his district and in the world in general?"

She chuckled. "Something like that. After the first year, working and going to school was too much to handle, so I quit and finished law school on some of the money Daddy left in trust. I've been in practice for two years now."

Reid leaned back and inspected her with appraising eyes. "A lawyer now? Loren, you're amazing! But I shouldn't be surprised. You were much too smart to remain behind the scenes. I'll bet you're a terrific lawyer!" He was unabashedly enthusiastic at her accomplishments.

Loren basked in his glory, glad for some crazy reason that he approved. "I share a small practice with a friend from law school."

He raised his eyebrows. "Who, Mark?"

She edged the rim of the coffee cup with a finger. "No. Another woman. Althea Montgomery and I share the same interests in the law and a small office in Crystal City." She watched his brow wrinkle at the mention of the location, but he didn't comment on it.

Instead, he asked, "Same interests? What's that?"

She sipped slowly, then set the cup down and exhaled. "We specialize in women's legal problems."

He raised his eyebrows again. "Like?"

She shrugged. "Oh, desertion, physical abuse, child support, divorce, of course. You know, the legal difficulties women encounter in life."

Loren felt the inevitable curtain of hostility between them. It was thin, but unmistakable. Suddenly she and Reid were on opposite sides of the fence simply because they were male and female. However, she always encountered this feeling from men when they discovered what she

67

did. She was accustomed to this reaction. It's just that she expected . . . wanted . . . more understanding from Reid.

His tone was curt. "You mean, the problems that women have with their men." It was a cold statement.

She met his dark stare with a steady one of her own. "No, it's usually the problems women encounter when one party or the other decides to end the relationship. Whether it's the man who skips out, leaving her with the responsibilities of their relationship, or the woman who's trying to escape a physically abusing husband, it's the severance that usually causes the problems."

His ebony eyes bore into her. "Fighting a personal war, Loren?"

"What's wrong, Reid? Feeling the pinch of a little guilt?" The words just slipped out.

"Hell, no! What severed our relationship six years ago left me with no guilt! Regret, maybe, but no guilt!" He was extremely defensive, and Loren knew it was her fault. She hadn't intended to put him in that position. It just happened. Her subconscious was working overtime.

With a calm, quiet voice, in contrast to his outburst, she said, "As a woman, I'm interested in the injustices to other women. Part of the fault lies with the woman, some with her man, and the remainder is society's."

He listened quietly, then: "I'll agree with that. Spread the blame around."

"I'm proud that I'm able to help other women." She smiled wryly. "But, I'll admit, Reid, I suppose I do relate to some of my clients." She stood and began clearing the dishes from the table. Inside, she was amused. Was this action because of instilled notions of her "duty," or instinctive, or just a job to be done? Probably the former. Society's contribution. "I know what it's like to be left."

Reid's angry face drew near to hers. "You also know

what it's like to be loved, damn it! And I know what it's like to be refused!"

She glared. "Is that why you fell so quickly into marriage? Got your ego damaged? Wanted to prove something?"

"Damn you, Loren! You know that's not the reason."

She turned away from his angry countenance. "Well, I know what it's like to be left with the woman's burden of a relationship!"

"Woman's burden? What the hell are you talking about?"

She turned back and looked at him coolly. "I was pregnant when you left."

"Pregnant?" The words echoed in his mind, trying to sink in. "You were pregnant with my child and didn't tell me? Why, in God's name, not?"

"At the time you left I didn't know, actually. But, within a few weeks, I was sure."

"You carried my child, Loren, and didn't tell me?"

"There wasn't time."

"Time? I—I can't believe it!" He was obviously shaken. "Why didn't you pick up the phone and call me?"

"Because I aborted at six weeks." Her voice was steady, and her blue eyes hard. She had been alone and shed many tears. But no more.

"Abortion! My God, Loren, how in hell could you?" He grabbed her arms with such a forceful grip that, for a moment, Loren feared his strength.

CHAPTER FOUR

Loren tried to wrench free from Reid's powerful grasp, but found herself lifted almost nose-to-nose with him. She could feel his steady breath falling evenly on her face, while hers was an irregular rasping that caught in her throat. Her immediate fear of his masculine strength was replaced with cool anger. Reid wouldn't dare hurt her! Through clenched teeth Loren muttered, "I was all alone here in Washington. You were out in God-knows-where, Arizona, getting ready for your big wedding when I had the miscarriage!"

Reid shook her slightly, his breath hot on her face. "Miscarriage . . . abortion—which was it? Your choice of words is confusing."

"What difference does it make?" she spat resentfully. "You weren't here, didn't care what happened to me! Or our child!"

His ebony eyes cut into her, and he clamped his jaw tightly. A muscle flexed across the dark cheek as Reid shoved her roughly from him. Fury raged through him, affecting his formerly even breathing. "Of course, I cared!" he retorted. "Oh, Loren, how can you say that? You act as though you don't know me at all, when you actually know me better than any woman ever has! I . . . loved you! I trusted you!"

Her hands rubbed the throbbing forearms where he had gripped her. "Trust?" she stormed. "We don't know each other at all now."

"I can tell you this! If only I had known, if you had told me you were pregnant, I would have prevented a goddamned abortion!"

Loren's voice countered coldly, left that way from too many tears shed alone over the years. "No one could have prevented what happened, Reid. Even if you had been here . . . and cared. I told you that I miscarried, aborted naturally. I wouldn't have an abortion. *Couldn't!* Surely you realize that."

He turned to her, crumbling inside at her words. "Miscarriage?" The full implications rocked through him. "Loren, Loren, baby, I'm sorry." Suddenly his male voice was shaky, and he attempted to take her in his arms. He craved to comfort her, to hold her. But it was too late. She was stiff and cold in response. "I wish to God I had been here with you. More than ever, *mi amor.*"

Loren quivered inside at the sound of the old affectionate phrase. With effort she pushed his arms from her. "Please, don't, Reid. It's over now. Long time over."

Then another thought struck him. "What if . . . what if you had been able to carry my child, Loren? Would you *ever* have let me know? My own child!" His broad chest heaved with emotion, and he struggled to keep from touching her.

A vengeful smile curled Loren's lips, and she folded her arms across soft breasts. "Oh, you bet! I would have slapped you with a paternity suit so quickly! What a lovely wedding present that would have made!"

He sighed heavily as his hands knotted into impotent fists. "I wish you had, Loren. Oh, God, I wish you had."

Loren watched him carefully, almost vindictively. After

71

all, she had been through a lot of hell because of him. *Because of him?* Was that entirely fair? She had been a willing lover. Now he was saying he wished he had known about her tragedy. *Their tragedy.* He would have been here. Helped . . . shared . . . comforted. Should she believe him? She tried to explain, feeling that he deserved to know. "It all happened so fast. I was having some physical problems, which is why I stopped taking the pill. By the time I realized that I was actually pregnant, my condition had worsened. I thought my physical problems were emotionally oriented, caused by our separation. There was nothing to be done to prevent the miscarriage. The doctor assured me it was for the best. At the time I doubted it. But, realistically, I know he's right."

Reid looked at her silently, his eyes deep and sorrowful. Or was that what Loren wanted to see—sympathy, remorse, agony? They were all there. But they failed to give her the satisfaction she always thought they would. She had wanted to punish him as she had been punished. And yet Reid seemed quite shaken by the revelation. He appeared truly disconcerted by the idea that they could have produced a child, *if only*—but life doesn't depend on "if onlys."

Loren continued to explain, her tone dull. "I was so hurt that you would go directly from my arms to hers, that I couldn't think straight. The pregnancy was just another reason to hate you."

"Hate me?" Reid raised his dark eyebrows. "I don't . . . *can't* believe that, Loren."

She smiled ruefully. "I wanted to. It would have been easier if I could have despised you. But you know, I couldn't do that." Her voice trailed to a whisper.

His finger lifted her chin. "I didn't spend last night with

72

a woman who hated me. Or this morning." His crooked smile was half teasing, half serious.

Her modest grin matched his, allowing the crisp air between them to soften. "I guess I'm just a sucker for old love stories."

His kiss was gentle as he teased her lips. "Our love story is just beginning, baby."

She shook her head and moved away from him. "There are too many complications to our lives now, Reid. You have your father to care for and a very different life-style out West. I have my career here in Washington. Then, there is—"

"Mark?"

She sighed. "Yes, Mark."

"What is your relationship with him?"

She turned away. "We're supposed to get married sometime."

There was an uncomfortable pause, then Reid asked the obvious question. "Do you love him?"

Loren laughed dryly. "What difference does that make? Mark and I have many of the same interests. We get along nicely. And he's here in Washington. He understands me and my needs. I understand his."

Reid looked at her with hard, cold eyes. "What difference? It makes a hell of a difference, Loren! How can you think of marrying him if you don't love him?"

"I loved you once, and it didn't lead to marriage. I don't think love is necessarily a requirement!"

"How can you consider marrying one man when your love is for another?" His words cut into her.

Defiantly Loren shot back, "But it isn't! I don't love another!"

Reid stepped close, leaning toward her until she backed against the kitchen cabinet. When there was no place else

73

to go, he bent down and caressed her lips with his own. His hands rested on the cabinet above, but didn't touch her. When the brief, orderly kiss was over, his lips curled into a formidable grin. "Oh, Loren, you can't respond to my kiss like that and convince me you love another man."

Instantly his vicious methods registered and Loren furiously raised a hand to slap him. He caught her hand in mid-air, then, grasping the other one, pinned them both to her back, kissing her soundly again. With her arms so caught he pressed his own chest tauntingly against her arched, full breasts. Her body refused to fight his advances and continued to respond, despite her wishes. A tightness grew within her as his torment elicited the desired reactions from her. He could tell she still responded to him!

When he finally released her, Loren moaned angrily. "Damn you, Reid Mecena! You're a devil to manipulate me like that!"

"Guilty," he murmured against her cheek. "I just wanted you to see how explosively we react together, Loren. The combustible chemistry is still there, so don't deny it."

"Then I am the biggest fool of all! Please get out. Leave me alone to think and try to sort this out."

He released her hands, but stood gazing down, his eyes settling on her taut-nippled breasts for a brief moment. "Okay. I guess you do need some time. So do I. I'm staying at the Fairfax. I'll gather my things and be back later."

"No! You're not staying here! Not this time, Reid!" Her voice had a firmness that was unfamiliar to him.

"You don't want me here?" It was a little-boy tone, and she wanted to concur. But she wouldn't give in. Wouldn't let herself.

"No. I definitely do not! You . . . you can't!"

"Why? Does Mark stay here? Weekends? Did I take his spot last night?" There was a bitter hardness in his tone.

Loren propped her hands on her hips defiantly. "No, he doesn't stay here! But, I . . . well, I just won't have you living here. You can't step back into my life this easily. I need time. And space. We both do."

Reid moved away, reaching for his jacket, which was still hanging casually on the chair. "Maybe you're right, Loren. But I'll guarantee that you haven't seen the last of me."

She placed her hand on his muscular arm. "Reid, we both have a lot to consider. To think about."

He nodded curtly. "Yes, I suppose we do. Right now I'm only thinking about us. Loren, I want to see you. Soon. What are you doing tonight?"

"Mark and I usually go out on Saturday nights."

Reid winced, knowing the reality of the situation. He was now seeing another man's woman. *Loren was another man's woman. Damn!* He sizzled inside with the thought! "Can you cancel? Tell him you're still sick?"

Loren sighed, thinking miserably about yet another lie. "I . . . I suppose so."

His order was abrupt and cold. "Then do it. I want to see you tonight."

Suddenly Loren's conscience surfaced. "Reid, I don't think I can! I just can't continue to lie to Mark then spend the evening with another man!"

The awful truth settled in on Reid and gnawed at his gut. *He was the other man in Loren's life. The intruder! The villain! Oh, God, he hated the role. He wanted her . . . all to himself again.* He ground his teeth together before answering. "Then don't lie to Mark. Tell him about us."

75

"Reid." Loren's eyes implored, searching his ebony eyes for understanding. "You know I can't do that."

His hand cupped her chin. "Loren, I must see you. I just want to talk to you . . . get to know you again. Is that too much to ask?"

She shook her head silently. *No, that isn't too much to ask. I want it too!*

He smiled tightly. "That's-a-girl. I'll bring dinner. About eight. How does Chinese food sound?"

Loren sighed miserably. How could she possibly refuse Reid? She had never been able to. *Except once.* Loren's head nodded, barely perceptibly.

"Loren." His voice was a husky whisper. "I don't want to intrude on your life. Just tell me to go to hell if you don't want to see me again."

Tears filled her eyes at his words. How many times had she wanted to do just that? But she shook her head. "I want you to come, Reid."

"I won't impose anything on you that you don't want. Do you understand? No demands, Loren. We'll talk and . . . I won't spend the night again if you don't want me to." His hand caressed her cheek.

Loren colored softly as she remembered their previous night. She had been so willing! "I know, Reid. It's always been—"

His large warm hand slid around her neck, nestling in her thick hair. "I like to think it's always been mutual between us, Loren. From the first—"

"It has, oh, Reid, Reid . . ." Loren agreed huskily before his lips crushed hers. As his mustache brushed her lips, his stubble of a beard scraped her tender face. But Loren didn't care. One touch, one kiss, and both she and Reid knew she would be his for the night. And he would be hers, *forever.*

76

"I'll see you tonight," he promised when he finally lifted his head.

"Reid." She grasped his arm. "Mark and I are going to that dinner tomorrow night. Together. But I'll call and set it up so that you're welcome to come. Several members of the Interior will be there. The contacts may be beneficial to your lobbying cause.

"Thank you, Loren. Are you sure we can't arrange something for you and me?"

She pressed her lips together and shook her head firmly. "Mark and I are going together, and I can't cancel that."

"Can't lie again?" His eyes scanned her smooth hair, then settled on her blue eyes. There was a hint of amusement in his. "Just don't bring him home with you."

Her alarmed eyes met his dark, brooding ones. He winked and was gone. As Reid strode out to his car, a million thoughts swarmed in her head. Predominant was the notion that he was perhaps a dream, a figment of her imagination. *And that her dreams had finally come true!*

With surprisingly little effort Loren convinced Mark that she was too ill to spend the evening with him. It left her with an uneasy feeling. Perhaps she was getting too good at lying. She was filled with guilt; that is, until she saw Reid again. Then she forgot everyone. She didn't care how she managed to see him, just so she did!

When Reid arrived on her doorstep with two huge bags of groceries, she laughingly stepped aside. "What's all this? Are you staying a week?"

He smiled wickedly. "Might!"

"Oh, no, you're not!" She followed him into the kitchen. Reid's jeans hugged his slim hips and muscular thighs. His casual cream-colored linen shirt was devastatingly open at the neck to reveal curly dark hair. He placed the grocery

77

bags on the kitchen cabinet, then turned to drink in Loren's appearance.

Loren wore sporty white linen slacks and a navy pullover. One look at her happy smile, and they both knew she hadn't stewed for long over her lies to Mark. Their eyes met magnetically, agreeing silently. In another moment Reid had cleared the space between them, gathering her into his strong arms, kissing her soft brown hair. She pressed her head against his chest, inhaling his masculine, leathery fragrance, stirred by the throbbing of his heart against hers.

"We're just beginning, baby. I promise," he murmured earnestly against her ear. And she believed it, because she wanted to. Oh, God, how she wanted to believe his promises.

They spent the evening cooking and laughing together, just like old times. They shared the meal and a bottle of wine. They talked about wonderful memories and what the six-year separation had wrought in their lives. But they didn't mention the future. It was too nebulous, scary. It was something neither wanted to face right now. The present was marvelous together. *Together, at last.*

At the end of the evening, Loren didn't have the will, the desire, to ask Reid to leave. And so he didn't.

Reid paced the shiny Italian-tiled floor. The full-bosomed black-and-white-attired maid stopped before him with her tray, offering another tall gin and tonic. Without hesitation he replaced his empty glass and took the full one. He was obviously preoccupied and ignored the shapely young woman. With a petulant expression she sought admiration elsewhere.

Reid tore his brooding eyes away from the door and gazed over the crowd. They were gathered in small groups, drinks in hand, politely discussing politics. What else? They were a staid-looking bunch, each and every one thinking his or her job was absolutely crucial to the total system. Everyone in government believed that. Everyone in the whole damn city of Washington, D.C., was vitally important. Or so they thought.

Considerately arriving on time, Reid had introduced himself to Packston George, the host of this intimate little affair. Pac was independently wealthy, owning homes in L.A. and Miami. If they were comparable to this marble and tile edifice in Washington's fashionable suburb, they would more suitably be called mansions. He was the newly appointed Deputy Chief of the Interior and God knows what he knew about the Interior's problems. Ah, such was politics. Obviously Pac neither knew nor cared about Arizona's water problems. Reid had his work cut out for him and it would be an uphill battle.

His dark eyes again cased the columned entranceway. *Where is she?* Loren was coming tonight with Mark. She had made that perfectly clear, and Reid had reluctantly agreed. What else could he do? Now they were half an hour late for cocktails. Where in hell were they? What were they doing? Inwardly he groaned at the thoughts that tormented his imagination.

Reid wanted her here—and he didn't. He knew he would be jealous as hell to see her with another man. And yet, he, himself, had no claims on her. Deep inside, Reid admitted that these last two days and nights with her had been sweet heaven, after a long and wicked hell. It was like blessed ecstasy after a prolonged abstinence. *A six-year abstinence from Loren.* And he found that he cared for her much more than he had ever dared to admit.

A small commotion snapped Reid's attention to the doorway. An attractive, well-dressed couple was visible through the columns, and his heart pounded with the recognition. There she was! *Loren!* Smiling, shaking hands, leaning on her escort's arm. *Not so close, damn it!*

Loren stepped down the few steps into the room. Tiny pearls of light graced her ears, matching the long, creamy strand that draped between her breasts. Her dress was black and very chic. It was apparent that she belonged in this elite setting. Reid stared dumbly at her, as if he hadn't seen her in years, hadn't held her close only a few hours ago, hadn't loved her throughout the last two passion-filled nights.

She smiled graciously and extended her hand. "Reid! How delightful! I want you to meet Mark Manning."

What an actress! Thank God she didn't introduce Mark as "my fiancé." Her voice trailed into his range. ". . . my old friend, Reid Mecena. Reid's from Arizona and is here lobbying for the new water bill before Congress." She stepped closer to Mark.

Reluctantly Reid's hand moved from hers to a mannerly handshake with the rather tall man beside her. God! It was hard to do! He wanted the hand to be a fist—jammed right into Mark's solar plexis. How dare he touch *her!* "Nice to meet you, Mark." Reid forced a smile. This evening he would have to be a pretty good actor himself. He didn't dare let his loving gaze rest on Loren. Instead, he eyed the man by her side.

Mark Manning was tall, brown-haired, and dynamic. He had a strong handshake and kept his left arm possessively around Loren's waist. Reid hated him instantly.

"My pleasure, Reid. Are you related to the Senator Mecena from Arizona who was in Washington a few years ago?"

Reid nodded. "My father."

Loren smiled encouragingly. "The senator is in poor

health now, Mark. He lives on the ranch back in Arizona."

"Sorry to hear about your father, Reid. What part of Arizona?" Mark exhibited mild attention as he accepted a martini from the buxom maid's tray.

"Southern Arizona. Near Tucson," Reid answered, taking another gin and tonic. Briefly his eyes grazed over Loren. She was absolutely gorgeous in her slinky black dress, with that low-cut neckline.

Mark responded with growing interest. "I know that area well. IBM, Gates Learjet, Hughes, and the copper mines. Tucson is a growing city. Lots of potential there, I understand."

Reid raised his eyebrows. Maybe the man was actually familiar with the area. "I'm surprised you're so informed, Mark. Most people think that all Arizona has to offer is the Grand Canyon."

"I make it my business to know, especially the sun belt cities. I'm impressed with Arizona's utilization of resources."

Reid smiled grimly. "The potential and future of southern Arizona is in direct relation to our need for an adequate water supply."

"Couldn't agree with you more, Reid. I'll be glad to help you with this water bill all I can. I know a couple of people who will be invaluable to you."

Reid gestured with his glass and muttered, "I've met Pac here."

Mark chuckled. "No, not this group. These are the figureheads. I know the behind-the-scenes guys. They're the ones you need."

Reid nodded knowingly. "I would appreciate any assistance I could get. I represent over three hundred businesses and ranchers in Arizona. Our economy is dependent on this bill."

"It's your economy I'm most interested in, Reid. In fact, I have a small investment in a mining company south of Tucson. It's been suffering drastically the last few years, and I'd like to see some profits someday," Mark admitted.

Loren looked curiously at him. "I didn't realize you had stock in a mine there, Mark."

He turned to her impatiently. "Of course, darling. Don't you remember last year when I went out there for a week?"

She studied for a moment, trying to recall. "I don't—"

"You were probably in the middle of a case, darling, and don't remember," Mark offered in a slightly condescending tone. Then, turning to Reid, he explained, "Sometimes Loren gets so wrapped up in those damned women's cases, she doesn't know what the rest of the world is doing."

"Oh, really?" Reid cast Loren a curious glance. Actually he was heartened to know that Mark could be gone from Loren for an entire week, and she hadn't even missed him.

"Back to Arizona's water problems, Reid . . ."

Reid listened politely, but inside he was smiling. And the singular dimple revealed itself daringly to Loren for the first time that evening. Taking a deep drink, he seemed to relax somewhat. "I can't guarantee that the passage of this water bill will increase the profits in your copper mine, Mark. But without it I can assure you that the mines—as well as all of us—will eventually fold."

"It's that important?" Mark's eyes narrowed as he assessed Reid's words.

"Absolutely," Reid asserted.

"I'd like you to meet my partner, Reid. How about lunch tomorrow?"

"Sure," Reid agreed. Much to his chagrin, Reid was finding that Mark had the personal interest and connections with the right people to be of more help on the proposed water bill than anyone in the room. Worse yet, he was willing to help.

Mark spotted an acquaintance across the room. "Would you excuse me for a few minutes, please, Reid, Loren? I've got to see Sam about a case."

"Certainly, darling," Loren murmured with obvious relief in her eyes.

"Tell me about your law practice, Loren," Reid requested loudly as Mark left them alone. Then, steering her aside, his eyes traveled curiously down her bare back. "Nice dress. How is that thing attached?" he murmured closely.

"Rude!" Loren fussed teasingly.

He shrugged with a grin. "You *are* beautiful in that dress. But I'm somewhat jealous when someone else eyes your spine. Where the hell have you been? I waited here over thirty minutes for you!" Intense jealousy gnawed at him whenever he thought of her alone with Mark.

"Sorry, Reid. I hope you didn't feel too awkward. The car stalled on the way, and we had to leave it and call a cab."

"A likely story," Reid said in a muffled voice.

"Reid, you're awfully paranoid lately. What's wrong?"

"Oh, nothing. I just love to see the lady I spend my nights with on the arm of another man!"

"Now, Reid, you knew—"

"I know, I know. I'm the intruder here."

Loren sighed. "Reid, please. Don't make things more difficult than they already are."

"The only way I can avoid that is to leave town. And, now that I'm here, and have you in my arms again, I won't give up so easily."

"Reid—" Her blue eyes implored a warning.

He turned casually. "Oh, hello there, Mark. Loren was just telling me about her interesting practice."

Mark barely acknowledged the statement. Instead, a worried frown creased his brow. "I'm concerned about leaving the car for too long, Loren. That's not the best part of town, you know."

Smoothly Reid said, "Loren mentioned car trouble. It's not a good idea to leave a car unattended at night in D.C. Not if you value it."

Mark agreed. "The more I think about it, the more worried I am."

"Tell you what, Mark. You call a tow truck and I'll drop you off so you can accompany your car to the station. And you won't have to worry about Loren. I'll be happy to see her home," Reid offered with genuine enthusiasm.

"Oh, I couldn't ask you—" Mark started to object.

Reid held his hand up. "Think nothing of it. It's the least I can do. Give me your card, and I'll call your office in the morning. We'll set up lunch."

Loren's large blue-violet eyes moved from Mark to Reid's dark, assured countenance. Well, he'd seen to it that she wouldn't be bringing Mark home tonight! Of course, she wouldn't anyway. But now she and Reid would have another night. *Another love-filled night!*

CHAPTER FIVE

"Loren, I have to see you. My God, but you're elusive! Do you realize it's been almost a week?"

Did she realize! Loren's heartbeat increased at the sound of Reid's strong voice and she gripped the phone tightly. She had purposely kept herself occupied and unavailable during the week, thinking that throwing herself into her work would force him off her mind. *Wrong!*

"Hello, Reid! How have you been?"

"Damned busy. And you?"

"The same. How's your job going?"

"Great, thanks to Mark! We've met with his law partner and several other key people this week. It's all preliminary, of course. But we'll be working on a proposal and a little ad campaign. Some of these people have very clever ideas."

"Good. I'm glad you're heading in the right direction."

"Mark has seen to that. And, Loren . . ." He hesitated.

"Yes?"

"He's, uh, Mark's a nice guy."

She smiled. "I'm glad you approve. Feeling guilty?"

Reid's answer boomed confidently. "I'm not saying I approve of your relationship with him! And, hell, no! I don't feel guilty! I want to see you! Now! This weekend at the very latest!"

Loren laughed, loving the jealous sound of his voice. *Loving him.* "I have a late appointment Friday night and plans for dinner with Mark on Saturday."

He paused and she could hear his labored breathing. "Okay, I'll see you Sunday. There is a reception I must attend, and I'd like you to go with me."

She sighed. "Oh, Reid, you know how I feel about receptions."

"This one's special, Loren. Congress has approved Navajo Code Talkers Day to honor the Indians' contributions during World War Two."

"Navajo Code Talkers Day? You've got to be kidding!" She started to laugh.

The tone of his voice halted her. "No, Loren. I'm very serious. The Navajos devised a complex communications system that was never broken. They served in every combat arena in the Pacific, yet received very little recognition."

"Why is the government just now getting around to honoring them?"

"Beats the hell out of me! Forty years late, I'd say! In all fairness, there have been award ceremonies for the Code Talkers in the past. But ceremonies that revere the dead or recall the horrors of war are not the Navajo way. This time it's in Washington, and it will be special. Please come with me, Loren. I think you'll find it interesting. I'd like you to meet some of my friends from Arizona."

"This is important to you, isn't it?" she asked quietly.

"Very."

"Well, Reid . . ." She hesitated, and his enthusiasm swept her along.

"I knew you'd come, Loren! And you won't regret it. I'll pick you up about noon, Sunday."

"Noon? What time is the reception?"

"It's at three. But I want to see you, talk to you, spend some time with you."

"Okay." She laughed, anticipation already building inside her. Could she wait the two days until she saw him, touched him again?

Loren hung the phone up and sighed heavily. Her violet eyes stared pensively down the brown cobblestone street, remembering the times they had walked to the wharf and along the Potomac. Those had been carefree days when neither had worried about the future.

Now she was older and wiser and very aware of the pain this unfulfilled love could bring. Her predicament had weighed very heavily in her mind this week, and Loren had kept to herself. She had been too busy to see Mark, and felt the need to pull back from her intensity with Reid. She knew she was plunging down a never-ending shaft of involvement with Reid again. Try as she might, she couldn't help herself. And yet she couldn't help being wary of this renewed relationship with him. It had meant heartache before. It would again.

There had been so many years since they had shared their love, both of them had changed. It was inevitable. And now, they—she—needed time and space to explore those changes. They needed to get to know each other again, to decide which direction they wanted to go. Right now Loren wasn't even sure. She was positive of only one thing. She still loved him, after all these years. And it scared her.

In her mind the solutions to their love weren't easy. First, if she gave in to her love, would she just be setting herself up for pain and grief again? Would Reid simply leave again? Deep inside, even now, she knew the answer. He was in Washington for a limited time, lobbying for a bill that would be voted on in a month or so. Then he would be gone. Reid's major responsibilities lay a world away from the nation's capital.

The alternate solution to his leaving was far from reasonable to Loren. Thoughts of uprooting her entire life, everything she had worked for, everyone she knew, the career she had built, everything that was familiar, were certainly less than appealing. Worse yet, it was something she had vowed to herself never to do. She wouldn't break that vow six years ago and couldn't break it now.

But, suppose . . . just suppose, there was another solution. Strange thoughts milled around in her mind, but even they were unsettling. It was not the kind of life she would ever, *ever* choose. Or was it?

No! She just couldn't!

And yet, was it so different from what she was doing now? From her past relationship with Reid? Oh, no! She had a different purpose then. She had hope. And now? Was there no hope for them? Was this alternative life-style one she could live with? Possibly . . . if it were the only way she could have him, the only way she would ever see him. Occasionally.

Oh, dear God! Am I crazy? What am I thinking?

Loren walked the floor and raked loose strands of unruly tawny hair back from her lovely face. Agonizing images wracked her brain as she tried to sort them out and reach an equitable settlement. At least attain a solution she could live with. And yet the singular idea kept approaching her from all sides. The only way to have Reid, on both their terms, was to be his mistress!

Could she live like that? Live with herself? Be happy? Would she be satisfied to have him whenever he came to Washington? Was her love that strong? To reserve it just for him? At his whims? At hers? Maybe . . . maybe it wouldn't be so bad. She would have plenty of time to pursue her career, her own particular life-style. And still she would have his love, if only occasionally. Perhaps . . . perhaps it would work. Conceivably she would have no choice.

Loren trudged into the bathroom and adjusted the faucet. She dropped the violet caftan and gazed down at her slim form. She was proud of her ability to remain slender. But, then she had always taken good care of her body, almost as if she were saving herself. For what? Motherhood? Seemed unlikely. For whom? Reid? Possibly . . . in her heart.

And she had done just that. Except once. One disastrous night of intimacy with Mark. Loren had lamented with the secret knowledge that Reid was the only man with whom she could achieve complete fulfillment. And never again had she been available to Mark. She had even postponed their marriage . . . indefinitely. And now she knew that she would never marry Mark. With a ragged sigh Loren acknowledged that she would have to settle for being Reid's mistress.

She stepped inside the shower stall, letting the water rain on her head, her well-shaped shoulders, her full breasts, the slim hips and straight, firm legs. And her tears joined the spray that trailed her cheeks and body to wash away down the impartial drain.

During the next few days Loren vacillated between jubilance and anguish in anticipation of seeing Reid again. She couldn't seem to keep her feet on the ground, and she felt ridiculously like a young girl in love. Wild, giddy, inebriated!

Then Loren contemplated her bizarre solution to their love, and wondered if she should tell him. It was so unlike her, even in opposition to what she would recommend for her clients. And yet it was the idea of a solution—albeit a bizarre one—that kept her eagerly looking forward to a continued relationship with Reid. That, and the fact that she couldn't help herself!

Whenever she was with Mark, Loren couldn't resist comparing Reid's rugged virility with Mark's suave sophistication, Reid's sincerity against Mark's sarcasm, Reid's sensuous kisses to Mark's perfunctory efforts.

The man who met her at the door on Sunday was rakishly western. Loren couldn't deny his appearance was very anti-Washington, but she delighted in the way he looked. Reid was himself—different, special. And she loved him, loved the sight of him, the masculine fragrance he emitted, the virility of his touch. All of her femininity melted in his presence, and Loren desired him with deep aching the moment she saw him. She longed to throw herself wantonly against his rock-hard body. Looking at him now, she wasn't sure she could ever let him leave her again. But she held herself in check and reveled in his splendid appearance. His finely tailored gray jacket squared broadly across his shoulders but tapered narrowly to fit his waist. It fell casually open to reveal a luxurious slate-blue silk shirt, caught at the neck with an elaborately etched silver Concho western tie. The navy slacks hugged his slim hips and topped gray lizard boots. The old, scuffy boots were gone. These were impeccable and gorgeous. In fact, his total look was expensive and marvelous.

"Well, howdy pardner," she drawled with a grin.

Wordlessly Reid stepped inside her small historic town house, his ebony eyes never leaving hers. Within another breathless moment she was in his arms, inhaling everything that was Reid Mecena, drowning in his flood of kisses. It felt so good, so right to be with him, in his arms, absorbing his essence. Loren wanted to press him into every cell, into her very soul. Whatever the solution to

90

their dilemma, she knew she had to have him. Even if it was occasionally, she wanted him with her in her arms.

"I've missed you this week, baby," he murmured. "I can't tell you how good it is to see you. To be with you. You fill a void in my life."

"Somehow you managed very completely for six years without me," she answered wryly.

"There was always a void left by the lack of your sweet love, Loren. I didn't realize just how empty my life was without you." He sighed, his hand moving possessively over her soft breasts.

She cocked her head, not intending to sound curt. But honesty tinged her voice. "Why do you think you can step back into my life and just pick up that love again?"

"Oh, baby, I don't. I just—"

"Want me, I know," she finished bitterly.

He folded his arms across the expanse of his chest. "No! That's not so! Not totally! Do you want me to prove it?"

She glanced around at him, curiously amused. "How?"

"We'll spend the day together . . . and I won't lay a hand on you. I won't touch you again until you suggest it!"

She laughed aloud at his droll suggestion. "I don't think you can!"

"Of course I can, woman! Don't you think I have any willpower at all?" He stood defiantly, arms akimbo, legs spread apart.

Damn! He was masculine and handsome! Loren wondered if she had the willpower to resist him. "Of course you do, Reid." She giggled, delighted with his new approach. So, he would try to drive her crazy? Well, she could play the game too. "We'll see how you manage today, Mr. Mecena. This is a test!"

He crooked an eyebrow. "A test? For me—or for you?"

"For you, silly!"

"And the prize for the winner?"

"Your own personal satisfaction, of course!" Loren propped her hands on her hips.

Reid's hands slipped through her arms to lock around the back and pull her close. "There's only one thing that will give me complete satisfaction—"

"Now, Reid, you promised!" She grabbed his hands and brought them around to the front.

"Well, then, get your clothes on, woman! If I can't have you totally and completely, we certainly aren't going to hang around here!" He swatted her on the rear as she scurried upstairs to change from her violet caftan. Giggling like a schoolgirl, Loren realized that she was as bad as he. She had been prepared for his intense lovemaking and her own unequivocal reception this afternoon. So much that she hadn't even bothered to dress! But Reid had turned the tables on her. Just what in hell was he trying to prove? She threw open her closet doors.

Reid was engrossed in the newspaper when she returned, fully clad in a navy and white silk sundress. It was one of her summer favorites. The jacket was slung casually over one spaghetti-strapped shoulder and her hair was brushed back, tucked behind one ear with a silver clip.

Reid whistled admiringly. "You look fantastic! Maybe I'll rescind my promise, gorgeous!"

She wagged a finger teasingly. "Oh, no, you don't! It's too late now! The vow is made! Anyway, I'm all dressed!"

He stood up, expelling his breath slowly. "There is only one vow I want to make to you, *mi amor. . . .*"

But Loren was in no mood for seriousness and laughingly handed him the key before preceding him out the door. "Where to, Jeeves?"

"Hmmm? Oh, I don't know. What sounds nice?"

She smiled enthusiastically. "The country. Let's go out to the country."

He opened the car door. *"A sus ordenes, mi señorita bonita!"*

They drove along the beautiful George Washington Memorial Parkway, stopping first to walk across the bridge to the tiny island that served to commemorate Theodore Roosevelt. Here was the privacy they sought on the small, elusive island with its thick green growth of trees and underbrush. However, the steady stream of tree-top-skimming jets approaching the airport drove them away, along with all the wildlife that was supposed to find refuge there.

Continuing along the turnpike that followed the Potomac, they ended up at Great Falls, Virginia. They shared a Coke, then walked along the tree-shaded paths. This place, where the Potomac crashed and rushed among giant boulders, was like a different river from the one that lapped lazily along the wharfs of old Alexandria. They talked and teased, enjoying the warm summer day and each other to the utmost.

Loren found that Reid had not changed so much after all. He worked hard for what was important to him—his family, property, and homeland. She couldn't fault anyone for that. She felt the same way.

Reid was impressed with how much change had taken place in Loren. She had a remarkable amount of drive, her accomplishments were amazing, and she was still beautiful. Oh, so beautiful. They could have talked forever, but for the Navajo Code Talkers' reception.

They drove back into town in silence, each savoring the day and their precious little time together. A large gathering milled around the formal rose garden. Some of the Navajos looked uncomfortable but others were smiling,

93

shaking hands, making an effort to meet everyone there. Obviously it was a typical Washington reception and a politician's field day.

"I recognize the Arizona senators. And there's a representative from New Mexico," Loren whispered.

"Oh, yes," Reid agreed quietly. "Since the Navajo reservation lies in both states, they wouldn't dare miss this occasion. There's Arizona's governor, the mayor of Phoenix, and the governor of New Mexico." He pointed out the public officials until he spied a friend. "There's Fred Tepaca. Fred was a code talker in Bougainville. Come on, Loren. I want you to meet him. Interesting man."

Loren accompanied Reid as he introduced her to several friends from Arizona. There was a tremendous sense of patriotic respect among all who attended. Realistically Loren knew that the occasion was merely symbolic, yet it was also significant, as attested by the array of television cameras gathered near the podium.

The ceremony was very poignant. There were speeches and awards. Loren was particularly touched by an elderly woman who hobbled forward to accept a Silver Star posthumously for her son's valor.

Glancing about the crowd of somber faces, Loren noted tears in the eyes of many. Suddenly the impact of what Reid had said about the importance of this day, at least for these First Americans, struck her. Perhaps, as he estimated, this ceremony was better late than never.

With a final honor guard twenty-one-gun salute and singing of "The Star-Spangled Banner," the ceremony was completed. There were a few brief moments of uneasy silence as everyone wrestled with memories of war and suffering and losing loved ones. Then the band struck up some refreshing popular music and the subdued group began to socialize and line up for punch and finger sand-wiches.

While Reid conversed with local officials about his work on the water project, Loren strolled around the elegantly landscaped grounds. She spotted an elderly lady sitting alone beside a magnificent yellow rosebush. Her brown skin and dark hair drawn back severely into a bun con-trasted with the vivid summer garden about her. There was a certain sadness in the lonely stare of the ebony-dark eyes and Loren was drawn to her. Walking closer, Loren recognized the woman as the one who had received a posthumous award for her son.

"Would you like some punch?" she ventured.

The woman stared at Loren with dark, unblinking eyes for a long moment, and Loren tried again. "Let me bring you something to drink."

The old woman blinked and a slight nod accompanied the gesture.

Loren was nonplussed by the initial unfriendliness of the elderly woman and returned a few minutes later with a small tray laden with drinks for them both, plus a variety of sandwiches and cookies. Together the two women ate and drank quietly. Loren finally introduced herself and the old woman did the same. Her voice was cracked with age, but there was an underlying strength of character that emerged as she spoke.

"I am Emmaline Walker."

"It's nice to meet you, Mrs. Walker. Are you from Arizona?"

The smooth, dark head nodded solemnly. "I travel from Bisbee."

Loren had no idea of the location of the town. "Is that near Tucson?" she asked hopefully.

Emmaline Walker nodded. "South."

95

Loren found it difficult to talk to the woman, who spoke in abbreviated, heavily accented syllables. "So you traveled from Arizona to receive this award in honor of your son? You should be very proud of him."

The woman shook her head slowly. "I did not travel this whole way to get a star of silver for my son who is dead."

"Did you come alone?"

"My daughter send me to talk to someone about what they call 'benefits.' But no one will listen. The men . . ." She stopped and waggled her old, wrinkled hand toward the politicians who stood talking earnestly, Reid among them. "The men are too busy with important things to listen to old woman. So I return with only this silver, which is nothing for the life of my son. But benefits will not bring him back either." She sighed and hushed.

"What benefits?" Loren was curious and leaned closer to catch each broken phrase.

"None."

Loren paused. "None? You mean the benefits stopped coming?"

The old woman spoke slowly. "The benefits not come."

Loren stopped in mid-bite. "Are you saying that you never received military benefits after your son's death? No monthly checks? No insurance money?"

The old woman blinked and nodded placidly. "None. And my granddaughter say I should get benefits from the government."

Loren sat up straight, realizing that she must gather more facts before taking any action. "Mrs. Walker, did your son die in the war? Was he killed in battle?"

"No fighter. Benjamin was code talker." Her voice was proud.

96

"Tell me about him. Please. I'll listen to your story, Mrs. Walker."

The old woman turned to look into the blue eyes of the young woman sitting beside her. "But you are only woman. How can you help?"

Loren knotted inside at the derogatory words, and if they had come from anyone else, she would have jumped to her feet and defended every inch of her femininity. Instead, she clamped her jaws and explained patiently, "I am a lawyer and I know about the laws that deal with the benefits you're supposed to receive."

"Anglo laws?"

Loren nodded. "Yes. Anglo laws. Please tell me about your son. What was his name?" She scrambled in her purse for a pen and scrap of paper, writing furiously as the old Indian woman related her tale.

The boy was eighteen when he was selected to be a marine from a boarding school in Shiprock, New Mexico. The group of intelligent young men was chosen specifically to be trained in the highly complicated code using the Navajo language. By the time he had finished communications training at Camp Pendleton, he was all of nineteen. He was shipped to the South Pacific without a visit home and, in the fall of 1943, Mrs. Walker was notified of his death on a faraway beach called Saipan.

"Didn't you know that you should receive military benefits after the death of your son?" Loren asked gently.

Emmaline Walker shrugged. "My husband was very bitter. Angry. He did not want any money for my son. Soon we moved to Bisbee so he could work in the mines. Now my husband is dead too. My daughters say I should have benefits."

Loren nodded thoughtfully. "I'm sure there was an insurance policy issued on your son. It's not much, but

. . ." She looked into the dark, sad eyes of the old woman and knew that even a small amount of money would help her. Pride had prevented her from any mention of money, preferring to call it benefits, and Loren understood.

"Loren! There you are!" Reid's voice broke into the women's privacy.

Loren looked up, suddenly aware that she and Emmaline Walker had been lost in the tragic story of Benjamin Walker, young Navajo code talker and hero, and the equally tragic tale of his mother's poverty.

"Reid." Loren smiled. "I want you to meet my new friend, Emmaline Walker. She is from Bisbee. Mrs. Walker, this is my friend, Reid Mecena. He lives in Tucson. His father was a senator."

The old woman nodded politely to him, but didn't speak.

Loren attempted to explain her concerns for the woman beside her. "Mrs. Walker tells me the tragic story about her son, Benjamin, who was a Navajo code talker. He didn't return from the battle at Saipan, and she never received his military insurance."

Reid stooped beside the bent old woman and took her weathered hand in his. "I'm sorry to hear about your brave son, Mrs. Walker. But there must be something we can do about that insurance. Let's talk to your congressman. He's here today." Reid gestured toward a well-dressed white-haired man who was conferring with a group of Navajo men.

Stubbornly she shook her head. "No more talking today. I try to tell my story to—them." She aimed her wrinkled hand vaguely. "But they did not want to hear old woman. This lady with blue eyes is only one who listens."

Reid smiled proudly at Loren. "Mrs. Walker, this lady is a lawyer. And if anyone can help you, she can."

Emmaline Walker nodded solemnly, accepting his words as fact. She showed neither elation nor hope, her face remaining placid. "I go now." She pointed toward the gathering of her associates, who were boarding a chartered bus for the journey back to their hotel.

Loren raised her eyebrows at Reid, then decided to make the offer anyway. "Let us take you back to your hotel, Mrs. Walker. Reid?"

"Of course. We'd love to. Give me a few minutes to get the car." He headed across the garden, stopping along the way to speak to the bus driver, informing him of their intentions to escort Emmaline Walker to the hotel.

After discovering that Mrs. Walker had foregone the scheduled all-day tour of Washington, Reid drove her around the Mall and Capitol. They paused where the woman showed special interest—the colorful flower gardens and formal shrubbery, which were rarities in her near-desert world. She was enthralled by the common sight of such shade trees as oaks and magnolias, and delighted Loren with her honest appreciation.

As they pulled in front of Mrs. Walker's hotel, Loren pressed her card into Emmaline's hand. "This card has my name and phone number on it. If you can think of anything else to tell me about your son, please call me. I will be back in touch with you, Mrs. Walker. And we'll do something about your benefits, I promise." She smiled reassuringly.

The old woman ran her finger over the embossed letters on the card. "Thank you for hearing an old woman's story."

Reid opened the car door.

Before she accepted his assistance, Mrs. Walker pressed a small box into Loren's hands. "This is yours, for listening. Now my daughters will be happy."

"Thank you," Loren mumbled as the woman took Reid's arm. "I'll get right to work on this." Absently she gazed down and opened the box in her hands. A painful exclamation escaped her opened mouth, for there lay the gleaming Silver Star! "Oh, no! I can't—" Her blue-violet eyes glistened, and she scrambled after Mrs. Walker.

However, Reid stopped her, placing his hand on her arm and pushing her gently away.

"But, Reid—" she protested.

His dark eyes met hers, and he shook his head, then turned his full attention to Emmaline Walker, who hadn't even noticed Loren's approach.

Loren watched helplessly as they walked slowly away from her. Reid's strong arm offered able assistance to a proud but aged Navajo woman. It was a beautiful sight. She turned her sad gaze back to the gift in her hand and salty tears dropped on the Silver Star.

When Reid returned to the car Loren had wiped the shiny metal clean. She was clearly upset about the gift and with Reid, besieging him immediately. "Why didn't you let me return this? Do you know that she gave me her award? Why would she do such a thing? I can't keep this! You know I can't keep this Silver Star that was given for her son's bravery!" Tears filled her eyes, and Loren felt very close to losing all control.

Reid's arms encircled her shoulders, and she felt his warm understanding and compassion. This was something she had needed at times from Mark, but had never received. Reid's voice vibrated through her. "I know, I know, Loren, honey. Mrs. Walker put you in a difficult spot. But you've got to understand this situation from her perspective."

"And you do?" Loren sputtered.

"Not completely," he hedged. "But I can tell you it would have been an insult to return the gift to her. You see, many of the older Navajos still believe that any reminder of a person who has died is taboo. Therefore, she looks at this award differently from the way you and I do. So it wasn't anything more than a silver gift to you, someone who showed her kindness. She gave it in good faith."

"But, Reid, I can't keep this," Loren protested again.

His hand caressed her cheek. "Maybe we can return it to her family someday. I'm sure her daughters would value it."

Loren blinked, trying to understand this woman who was so different from her. "Poor Emmaline Walker. Caught between two cultures in a typical government snafu, and no one would listen to her."

"Loren, you're amazing," Reid said quietly. "In that whole group of people today, there was one woman who needed you, and you managed to find her! I'm proud of you!"

She smiled wanly, feeling better with Reid beside her, giving the support she needed. Shrugging, Loren admitted, "It just happened. I really wasn't looking for her. Actually Mrs. Walker had given up on finding anyone who could help. When she said that the men wouldn't listen to her, my ears perked up."

Reid kissed her lips quickly, then started the car. "You're wonderful. And you seem to have found your niche."

Somehow her answer came out more defensively than she had intended. "I have worked very hard for 'my niche,' as you call it. The journey was not easy. And I don't intend to give it up."

Her words echoed in the close quarters of the car, and they drove on in silence. Loren wondered why she had said such a thing.

Reid pressed his lips together, pondering her words, knowing the inherent difficulties they represented.

CHAPTER SIX

Reid's rented car sped along the highway as he crossed the river and drove north into Maryland. The lush foliage on either side formed an avenue of deep green of a richness Reid had forgotten in the years since he had been there. The fresh, moist fragrance filled his nostrils and seemed to pervade his entire body, stirring dormant emotions. The heavy growth of trees, the thick green vines growing wildly, the humid, briny air off the bay, the times with Loren, all filled his memory with excitement. He was meeting her today in one of their old favorite haunts. He could hardly wait to see her again. It had been two weeks since their last time together. It felt like eons.

Reid wheeled off the main highway, and after several miles turned again onto the small road that seemed to head back in time. Its narrowness was emphasized by huge water oaks that tunneled the old road. There was a definite saltiness in the air now. He could smell it, and it aroused a distinct longing for her. He was close to his destination.

Then he spotted it. The small shanty was seemingly a hundred years behind the times, and a hundred miles from anywhere. It had been a wonderful place to escape to, years ago, when it was only the two of them in the world that mattered.

Reid pulled to a stop in front of it and smiled faintly at

the weathered plank nailed over the doorway, claiming simply RESTAURANT. Loren's car was already here, and he knew where to find her. He inhaled the damp, salty air and something kindled inside him. Reid knew he had to have her again, and he couldn't leave her this time. With long strides he avoided the front door, heading knowingly around to the back, to the small balcony porch that overlooked the inlet.

And there she was! Reid's heart pounded at the sight of Loren, sitting alone at the crude wooden table, looking out over the rippling water. He was filled with love and longing for her that six years and worlds of differences had not been able to obliterate.

"Why don't we skip lunch and go someplace secluded," he murmured against her ear, his hot breath tickling her neck.

"Hmmm, what a romantic idea." She turned to him with a happy smile. Their eyes locked for a moment in time and their love was obvious.

Her hand reached up to caress his face and pull it possessively toward hers. Loren kissed him gently and lovingly. "Isn't this secluded enough for you? I wondered if you would even remember how to get here. It's been so long."

Reid scooted his hips next to hers on the wooden bench and took her hand. His lips and that devilish mustache played over her knuckles. "Remember? Ah, *mi amor,* after all the time we spent here and around this bay? My heart remembers, Loren. I was serious about getting away, alone. I'm aroused just looking at you. It's been two weeks since—"

"I know how long it's been, Reid."

"You do?"

"Of course. I miss you, too, when we're not together."

"I miss your gorgeous body!"

"Reid—" Loren gasped, blushing slightly.

"Without you I'm miserable, Loren. Not to mention unsatisfied!" His teasing eyes were alight with passion, and he looked questioningly at her.

Their rapt attention was broken when the waiter set a tall gin and tonic before Reid.

"I ordered a drink for you. Hope you don't mind," Loren explained.

"Fine." He nodded curtly to dismiss the waiter.

"Reid, why don't we go ahead and order?" She squeezed his hand affectionately. "I have an appointment with a client in an hour."

Loren had answered his question and, at the same time, crushed his hopes for an afternoon rendezvous.

Reid sighed and gave her a wouldn't-you-know glance. "Okay. What'll you have?"

"A soft-shell crab sandwich," she announced with satisfaction, then turned to Reid. "Try it. It's great!"

He raised his dark eyebrows. "Crab? No thanks. I'll have a hamburger."

When the waiter had left, she explained. "Reid, I'm sorry. It's just that I have a lot of work to do this afternoon. Several appointments."

"I can tell you're a career woman. You can't even take time out for a little fun," he admonished, his dark eyes teasing.

"I took the time to come all the way up here for lunch with you, didn't I?" She sipped her own half-empty gin and tonic.

"Yes," he admitted. "And I'm glad you did. I must admit, I've been wondering why."

Loren sighed and looked out over the water. The salty breeze lifted her tawny hair away from her face. "I

105

. . . sometimes I come up here alone. Just to reminisce and enjoy. But always alone, because this was our place, Reid. And I just wanted to remember it again, with you this time."

"It has been a long time since I've been here, but it seems the same. Unchanged. It's beautiful, and just being here turns me on to you something fierce!" He nuzzled her earlobe. "I'd like to think our love is unchanged, too, Loren."

"Oh, Reid, nothing stays unchanged." She quivered inside at his touch, his kiss, his admission of love. She knew it, and felt it too. But—

"Maybe you're right, Loren. Actually I had another reason for calling you up today for lunch." His voice was low and serious. "I got a call this morning from home. It's my father. He's very ill."

"Oh, Reid, I'm sorry," she said, covering his hand with hers.

"I need to go back to see about him, Loren. And I want you to go with me. I'm going to wind up some business this afternoon and leave early in the morning."

"Reid, I . . . can't. I have too many things to do this week."

"You'll have this afternoon to cancel them and make other arrangements. Please come, Loren. I have always wanted to show you my world. This is your chance. It won't cost you a thing. I'm flying my plane and—"

"Your plane?"

He nodded. "Sure. It's the easiest way to get around these days. Wouldn't you like to go with me, Loren?"

"Yes, but—"

"Then figure out a way. It will be a mini-vacation for you. And a chance to see my world." His tone was decisive.

"Your world?" she laughed. "You make it sound like another continent."

He looked up at the thick-leaved branches draped over the lazy river. "It almost could be, Loren. It's very different from all this."

"Reid, I just don't see how I can go. I have appointments all week, and—you will be back, won't you?" Her large eyes rose alarmingly to him. She wasn't ready to lose him yet.

He shrugged. "Depends on Dad's condition. My work here isn't finished. I'd like to stay longer, make more contacts. I plan to return in a few days."

"I am sorry about your father, Reid. But I wish you didn't have to go. I'm afraid you won't return." She dropped her eyes and dark lashes feathered her cheeks.

"Then come with me. Don't make me go alone. I—I just want you with me, Loren." His finger lifted her chin while his thumb edged her lower lip longingly.

Her eyes met his, and she knew there would come a time when his work in Washington would be finished. And then—*what*? "Oh, Reid, don't make me choose now."

"All I want you to do right now is go to Arizona with me."

"I . . . well, maybe," she mumbled, then a flicker of light touched her eyes. "Maybe I could make it a partial business trip."

"What business?"

"My business! With Emmaline Walker! Could we visit her?"

"Emmaline who? Oh, you mean the Navajo woman we met."

"Yes. I have her benefits straightened out and was just about to write her a letter. But I'd rather deliver the message in person! And I want to return her Silver Star."

"Great! Fine! Whatever you say! Just so you go along!"

"Can you take me to Bisbee? Is that near Tucson?"

"Sure," he shrugged. "No problem. We can handle it. I'm going to show you another world, Loren. I hope you'll enjoy it."

"Oh, I know I will. What should I wear?"

"No business suits!" he warned, and they both laughed and shifted as the waiter placed sandwiches before them. Even this secluded place was too public for them.

Reid's dark eyes were riveted to Loren's sandwich. "What the hell is that?" Scraggly bits of the contents were visible between thick slices of bread.

Loren glanced down at the item, then back up at Reid with the most innocent expression she could muster. "A soft-shell crab sandwich. Want a bite?"

He cringed in mock horror. "A *what*?"

She giggled. "It's a crab that's caught while molting. These have no shell and are deep fried. They're delicious! Here, try it!" She generously offered her lunch.

"No! No, thank you!"

As if to prove her bravado, Loren took a bite. "Hmmm, they fix the best crab sandwiches here! I think it's the sauce . . . or the fresh—"

"Loren, what is this?"

"Just a crab leg."

"That's what I thought." Reid eyed the food as if he thought it would hop out onto the table.

"Don't look at it, or imagine anything, Reid. Just take a bite and enjoy the flavor." She leaned toward him. "You do like crabs, don't you?" It was a question that fell into the baseball, motherhood, apple pie, and Maryland's crabs category.

He pursed his lips. "I've had a few steamed crabs with

108

beer, but it's not my favorite form of food." He still hadn't touched his hamburger.

"Oh, for God's sake, Reid, try it!" She challenged him by holding it inches before his mouth.

There was no easy way out, so he took a bite. For one brief, frantic moment he thought the whole thing would return to embarrass them both! Mustering all his fortitude, Reid managed to chew the crunchy things in his mouth and swallow.

Meanwhile Loren was laughing heartily at his facial expression. "Reid, you're positively green!"

"You will pay for that, young lady," he warned with a threatening gleam in his eyes.

She shrugged. "I don't see what all the fuss is about. It's totally cooked."

"The *whole* thing?"

She nodded reassuringly. "The whole thing."

"All of it? *All*?"

"Of course," she smiled.

"I think I'll stick to hamburgers," he muttered, taking a huge drink of the gin and tonic.

"I can't believe you didn't like that, Reid. I was just sure—"

"I'm the one who doesn't like seafood, remember?" he grated.

She smiled sweetly and reached over to caress his face. "Oh, Reid, I remember. I remember . . ." she whispered.

They finished eating and strolled down by the narrow river, content to be together in their little place that time forgot. Just to be together was so wonderful, so fulfilling, they could almost forget the outside world and all the problems that tugged at them. Almost . . .

"Reid, I must get back to work. I have appointments all

afternoon. And I need to check with Althea to see if she can handle the office alone this week."

He sighed. "Yeah, I know. I need to check with the airport and see if everything's in order for our trip tomorrow. I'm hiring a mechanic to make sure the plane's in shape for a three-thousand-mile trip. We're leaving very early, around dawn."

She nodded and slipped her hand into his as they ambled back to the cars. "Reid, what about your father? How is he?"

"He's been hospitalized in serious condition. Lupe says he has a lung infection. Trouble is, he's just not strong enough to fight these infections anymore. Everyone at home is very upset, and I need to be there."

"This won't be a very pleasant trip home for you. Are you sure you want me tagging along?"

They halted between their cars. "Positive. Having you there will make it bearable. And give me some lovely diversion."

She smiled. "Reid, why don't you come over tonight? We can leave together early in the morning."

He cast her a grateful look. "Sounds like a reasonable, practical plan."

She nodded pragmatically. "I'll see you later then. And thanks for meeting me here for lunch. I've loved it."

Reid grasped her forearm and pulled her against his chest. "Loren, I love you." His whisper rocked through her as if he had shouted it to the world.

"I know," she acknowledged, and let her lips enjoy his brief caress. Then they both drove back down the highway to the bustling city.

As darkness fell, a full moon bathed the capital city, the Potomac, and the little town house on Prince Street in its

110

luminous splendor. Inside, that glow was enhanced as Loren basked in Reid's loving arms.

Reid's head and shoulders rested on a pillow against the brass headboard, and he cradled Loren's slender form against his golden muscles. His tanned hand contrasted with her cream-colored breasts while his thumb teased the tip to berry ripeness. He caressed her rib cage, waist, and hips, then rested his hand on her rounded buttocks. Occasionally he tugged her to him.

"Did you tell Mark you were going to Arizona with me?"

"What a thing to think about at a time like this! What's wrong? Feeling guilty?" She traced lacy figures in the dark mat on his chest.

"Not exactly guilty. It's more like a burning rage inside me whenever I think of you two together or see that goddamn ring on your finger." His voice was a growl that vibrated through his bare chest and into Loren's being. She could feel the strength of his feelings on the subject.

Immediately sitting up, she extended her left hand. "Does this make you feel any better?" With a deft, sure motion, Loren removed the engagement ring and tossed it casually onto the dresser.

"Loren—" He grasped the ringless hand and pressed it to his lips, his mahogany eyes imploring, questioning.

"Reid, you're right about Mark and me. We don't belong together. I—I just can't wear his ring any longer."

"Do you think if I hadn't reappeared in your life you and Mark would still have gone your separate ways?"

She hesitated and her blue eyes met his honestly. "I don't know, Reid. But I am sure that if I continued with this mockery of a relationship with him, it would be a mistake. It's you I love . . . always have. No matter what happens, I will always be yours."

111

Before the last word was out, his lips crushed hers. A low moan of undisguised longing escaped Reid's throat, and he clutched her to him as if he would press her into every cell, as if he would never let her go. And, indeed, Loren wanted to be his forever. Wanted them to be together, like this, forever.

It was a kiss like none other—the first passionate kiss between lovers . . . the last lovers' farewell . . . as if they had never loved, and lost . . . wonderful and desperate and compelling. Forever enduring. Loren met Reid passion for passion, strength for strength, lips to merging lips, tongue to exploring tongue, love for enduring love.

When the impact of the kiss had left them both breathless, Loren slumped back against the pillow while Reid rained feather-light kisses over her upturned face and eyelids and flushed cheeks. His lips found the hotly pulsing hollow of her neck, then caressed the creamy mounds of her breasts, pausing to tug gently on each ripened peak. She arched to meet his pleasure, and he obliged with a lingering, gentle sucking motion for each rose-tipped mound. A kittenish purring told him she was ready for more, and he was only willing as he traced her navel with his tongue before plunging inside.

She dug her hands into his dark hair, pulling him achingly to her as he prolonged her agony with soft nips on her sensitive inner thighs.

"Reid, please—"

"Loren, Loren, don't ever forget . . ." He slid over her, his burgeoning manhood hot against her. "I love you."

They were the last gasping words she heard before they both plunged into the exploding peaks of passion. The moments hung like golden threads in time, binding them together forever. Loren would always cherish his vow spoken in the throes of love's highest frenzy.

112

As the burning embers inside them cooled, Loren could feel Reid slipping from her. She clutched him in a futile attempt to hold on to the man she loved.

"Oh, Reid, Reid, I love you so much. Never leave me."

His voice was muffled against her neck. "Our love is too strong, *mi amor*. I won't leave you. I can't."

Sudden tears filled her blue eyes. "Reid, what's going to happen to us? Will we—"

His shadowed face hovered near hers in the darkness. "We'll work things out, Loren. I promise. I will always love you. My desire for you hasn't diminished since the first time we made love."

To prove it, he made love to her again and held her to him throughout the night.

The early fingers of dawn found Loren curled in the secure nest of Reid's arms. She wondered, in her dreamlike state, what his "world" would be like. She knew Reid so well, yet she didn't. There were still unanswered questions. Deep inside, she worried about their future. Was there a place for them to be together? Was this wonderful time in his arms limited? If she declared herself his mistress and reserved her love just for him, would he return often to see her? To love her? Could she even bear living like that?

Reid sighed in his sleep and nestled his head against her neck. Loren shivered at the chilling thought of losing him again.

The trip across the country in Reid's twin-engine Beechcraft was a delightful experience for Loren. The weather was perfect, and they pointed out familiar landmarks to each other. As they traveled farther westward, Loren recognized less and less of the land.

Flying over Texas, Reid teased her. "That hill looks familiar! No, I believe it's that one! Or maybe . . ."

Loren laughingly joined his banter. "How could you tell? They all look alike from up here!"

"The only way I could really tell which is *our hill*"—he paused and cleared his throat—"is to try them all out!"

"Oh, clever idea, Reid." Loren chuckled. "We'll never arrive in Arizona!"

"You're right. We don't have time to stop now." His dark eyes caught hers and his tone was suddenly somber. "Do you remember those days, Loren?"

"Yes, I remember," she said quietly.

Silently they recalled the days when their love had been so easy, and neither had thought of parting. He had called her up with the notion that they were flying to Texas with his family. He had something special to show her. Loren was so excited, she had gone right out and purchased a new pair of jeans.

They had flown in the family's Beechcraft to a friend's ranch west of Austin. It was a ranch like none Loren had ever seen. The landing strip on ranch property was lined with several single- and twin-engine planes. There was a huge swimming pool, tennis courts, and a large central house with adjoining smaller guest houses. Reid had bought Loren her first cowboy boots, and that night introduced her to country swing and the Cotton-eyed Joe. They had danced until the wee hours of the morning.

The next day they had driven around the lakes north of Austin. Loren had never seen such magnificent flowers as those highly touted bluebonnets that covered the hills. There were millions of them. She and Reid had found a secluded place and made love. After all, he had promised . . .

"Your eyes are still that color, *mi amor.*" Reid's voice

114

rumbled into her daydreams above the sound of the plane's motor.

Loren turned her blue-violet eyes to him. "How did you know what I was thinking?"

"When are you going to admit that we're on the same wavelength? I know what's going on in that head of yours because it's going through mine too."

She smiled enigmatically and tried to swallow the knot in her throat. Loren couldn't help but wonder if he knew everything that had trailed through her muddled mind in the last few weeks since his reentry into her life. He just couldn't possibly know what she was wrestling with.

There was nothing in Loren's past, nor in all the travel books, nor in all the *National Geographics*, nor in Reid's descriptions, to sufficiently prepare her for the sight of the Arizona landscape.

"Welcome to Cañada del Oro, *mi amor,*" Reid said as they rolled to a halt on the runway. "There's Raul waiting for us!" He pointed past the plane's wingtips to see a dark-skinned, robust man waving beside a jeep.

Beyond Raul was the very strange world of Reid Mecena. Cacti of various shapes and sizes dotted the lean landscape, along with small pale green bushes and an occasional clump of grass. Some of the cacti appeared deceptively fuzzy as the rays of the evening sun reflected a yellowish glow around them. However, the most unusual plants Loren had ever seen were the huge saguaros. They stood taller than a man and almost as big around, lifting armlike branches upward. Some of the branches even curled back as if to wave or beckon.

"*Bienvenida, señorita.*" Raul greeted her warmly as he helped her down the wing-step. "Welcome to Arizona."

The first thing she noticed as her feet touched the earth

115

was the heat. "Thank you. You must be Raul," Loren said.

"*Sí,*" he admitted, then turned his attention to Reid, who was rounding the plane. "Señor Reid!" They shook hands and hugged at the same time, clapping each other affectionately on the back.

"How's my father, Raul?" A look of concern creased Reid's tired face.

Raul shook his head sadly. "*Está malo,* Señor Reid. Señor Mecena, he is very bad."

The morose statement cast a pall over the small group as they unloaded the luggage and tied the plane securely. Although the area was desert in appearance, the land was not flat. Huge bare mountains loomed on either side of the dirt road they traversed to Casa del Oro. The sprawling adobe brick house seemed to be set into the side of the mountain, although, as they pulled closer, Loren could see that it wasn't. She caught glimpses of brick walkways and enclosed patios all around the house. She was quickly ushered, amidst a smattering of Spanish and a great deal of rapid English, to an open veranda that extended the length of the house. There she was offered a spectacular view of the desert floor for miles and miles.

Loren was introduced to Lupe, who hugged her, then thrust a tall glass of mint tea into her hand.

"*Es muy bonita,* Señor Reid," she murmured repeatedly. "Are you hungry? Here are some chips. And some fruit."

"Thank you, Lupe. I would just like to stretch a little," Loren said, walking down the Mexican-tiled veranda. "There is so much land here, I just can't believe it!" Prolific magenta bougainvillaea draped gracefully over every post the entire length of the long, covered porch. A stretch of brick walkways and stairs led down to a large swim-

116

ming pool. Except for the colorful inlaid tiles, the swimming pool appeared to be a natural, rambling expanse of water encased in grayish boulders. Beyond the pool the land sloped ever downward until it stretched into a desert valley several miles in width. There, on the horizon, loomed another craggy mountain range. The sun, a brilliant orange ball, hovered hotly over the cool purple mountain outlines.

His masculine hand settled comfortably on her shoulder as Reid murmured, "Beautiful, isn't it." He meant the words as a statement of fact.

"Why, Reid, it's breathtaking! And all this space—"

"Loren, do you mind if I go ahead to the hospital? Everyone around here is in such a turmoil, I need to see for myself exactly what Dad's condition is."

"Of course not, Reid. Do you want me to go with you?"

He shook his head curtly. "No. Dad is in intensive care and you probably couldn't see him anyway. You stay here and relax; try out the pool. I hope you brought some cool clothes."

"Oh, yes," she nodded. "And I think I'm ready for my skimpy sundress now! Please, Reid, go ahead and take care of your family. I'll be fine here."

"We should have a beautiful sunset tonight. Don't miss it!" He led Loren back toward the house. "Lupe, take care of Loren, *por favor*. And show her to my room please. I'll take the guest room. I'm going to the hospital to see about Dad now. I may not be home soon, so don't hold dinner."

Lupe nodded and began to gather Loren's things. "*Sí,* Señor Reid."

Reid kissed Loren quickly, then disappeared around the hacienda, leaving her to follow Lupe inside. Glass walls allowed the outside beauty to enter the living quarters, giving the feeling of being completely enmeshed with the desert. The cool house was definitely influenced by Mexico and the earthen tones of the Southwest.

The two women walked across expansive rooms, floored with large, square Mexican tiles. Mexican and Indian oil paintings hung on white brick walls. Huge, dark tables and large, comfortable-looking chairs constituted most of the rather crude furniture, by Loren's standards.

"This room is Reid's. I think he wants you to enjoy the view and the Jacuzzi," Lupe offered, showing Loren the magnificent bathroom that surrounded a beige-tiled Jacuzzi. The room was as big as her own tiny living room back in Washington!

"Oh . . ." was all Loren could manage as her wide-open eyes tried to take in everything.

"And this," Lupe explained as she opened floor-to-ceiling shutters, "is the view."

"Oh, my," Loren muttered inanely as words failed her. "It is lovely!" Sliding glass doors opened onto a small enclosed patio landscaped with natural desert plants. A tiny green-breasted hummingbird hovered near a barrel cactus bloom, then flickered away. Looming beyond the house and small patio were the granite cliffs of yet another mountain range.

"*Sí, señorita.* Yes," Lupe said. "It is beautiful."

"Oh, Lupe, this entire place is amazing! Why, this room is almost as big as my whole house back in Washington! And the bathroom—" Loren halted, lacking adequate words. Her eyes swept around the room with its huge bed adorned with a brightly colored coverlet, dark, bulky furniture, and expanses of glass walls.

"Yes, *señorita,*" Lupe responded politely, her dark eyes observing Loren's reactions.

"Please, Lupe, call me Loren. I've heard so much about

118

you, I hope we can be friends. Reid thinks very highly of you."

Lupe smiled at the mention of Reid's name. *"Gracias. I have heard of you, too, Señorita Loren. Reid told me about you. I'm glad you came with him this time."*

Loren raised her chin at the slight comment, wondering just how much Reid had told Lupe about them. "I'm glad I came, too, Lupe. It's beautiful here."

Lupe turned the covers down. "If you are tired, please feel free to take a nap. Dinner will be ready in about an hour. It will be simple tonight because"—she paused and sighed heavily—"the men aren't here."

"That will be fine with me, Lupe. Thank you." Loren slipped out of her shoes and began to think seriously about the pool.

Lupe smiled from the door. "You Anglos have a saying: 'Make yourself at home.' Out here we say, *Mi casa es su casa.* It means my house is your house.

Loren returned the warm smile, thinking that Reid probably meant it literally for her. "Thank you. I'm feeling very comfortable already."

"And, *señorita,* don't forget about the sunset. Señor Reid wouldn't want you to miss it."

Loren peeled off her clothes and searched her suitcase for her swimsuit. She spent the next few hours exploring the hacienda, the pool, the veranda and its spectacular view, the glorious sunset. She dined alone, sipping mild bean soup and nibbling crunchy tortilla pieces, overlooking the beauty of the quiet desert evening.

Occasionally lights twinkled, and Loren found herself nodding with fatigue. It had been a long day. Her intentions of staying up to wait for Reid faltered, and Loren decided that she could as easily see him in the morning.

Almost the moment her head touched the cool pillow,

119

Loren was asleep. Sometime in the night, she stirred to the warmth of a masculine body curling close, and Reid's familiar fragrance permeated her very being. She enfolded him in her arms and murmured, "I like your world, Reid."

"Did you try the pool?"

"Um-hum. Nearly froze!"

"The sunset?"

"Spectacular!"

"So are you." He buried his face against her neck.

"Reid, how's your father?"

His voice was a low groan. "Stable. We're waiting and watching."

"Oh, Reid, Reid . . ." She comforted him in a mellow voice, holding and stroking the masculine form pressed against her throughout the night.

The sun was squeezing through the shutters the next morning when Loren awoke. She gazed sleepily around the empty room and wondered if she had been dreaming again that she'd held Reid in her arms all night. It wouldn't be the first time such a vivid dream had been hers.

CHAPTER SEVEN

Loren was amazed at the coolness of the morning, knowing that the temperature would reach nearly a hundred by midday. She enjoyed a light breakfast of fresh fruit and a Mexican sweet roll with strong coffee. Afterward she roamed around the grounds by herself. On the way to the stables she scared up a large jack rabbit with towering ears. The horses were frisking around an enclosed field, obviously enjoying the early-morning coolness. She propped her arms on the fence railing and watched the quaint ambling of a roadrunner. He screwed his head all the way around and gazed curiously at her, then streamlined his strange body and ran away. A family of gambel quail, topknots bobbing, scurried out of sight.

She was still chuckling about the unusual animals she had seen when she approached the veranda.

"*Hola,* Señorita Loren," Lupe greeted her. "Would you like something else to eat? You didn't eat enough this morning."

"Oh, yes, I had plenty. Don't forget I sat in a plane almost all day yesterday! But I would like some hot tea. I'm very thirsty this morning."

"*Sí.* That's because it's very dry here on the desert. You should always keep drinking something. We have some beer, if you like," Lupe added with a grin.

"Oh, no," Loren chuckled. "Not now, anyway. Tea would be just fine for me. Let me come with you, and I'll fix it."

Lupe led the way into the kitchen, and Loren perched on a convenient stool. "Where's Reid?"

"Señor Reid has gone to the hospital this morning. Said he wanted to see the doctor when he went around." Lupe shrugged.

Loren stirred her tea and explained with a smile, "Most doctors make rounds every morning, very early. They check on all their patients in the hospital at that time. Sometimes it's the only time to talk personally with the physician."

"Oh." Lupe busied herself with chopping some vegetables. "Reid is very worried about his father. This has come at a very bad time for him, with the business he must do in Washington. Señor Mecena is a fine man . . . fine man." Her voice trailed off, and she shook her head as she worked.

"You're worried about Senator Mecena, too, aren't you, Lupe?" Loren asked with concern.

Lupe nodded silently. "*Sí.* He is so sick, I'm afraid he will—" She stopped and choked back a sob. She raised large, tear-filled eyes to Loren. "I'm sorry, *señorita,* I didn't mean to let you see me cry."

"Why not? Lupe, I understand your feelings. Go ahead and cry. Let go of your emotions a little."

Lupe looked doubtfully at Loren, wondering how this young woman knew so clearly how she felt inside. "He is more than a boss. He is a friend. *Es amigo.*"

"Don't be embarrassed, Lupe," Loren encouraged her gently. "Wouldn't you rather cry with me than when Reid is here?"

Large tears trailed Lupe's dark face, and she nodded.

122

"Oh, yes! He's got too much to worry about without a silly woman who sits around the kitchen wringing her hands and crying."

Loren smiled sympathetically and reached across the counter to pat Lupe's hand. "You aren't silly. And you certainly aren't sitting around wringing idle hands. A few tears will probably be good for you. How long have you worked for the Mecenas?"

"Twenty years. And *mi madre* before that. She helped take care of Señora Mecena before she died, and Reid was just a boy." She paused to blow her nose. "When I was old enough to help, they hired me too. Señor Mecena has been so good to me."

"I know you're grateful to him. He is a loving and kind man," Loren acknowledged gently.

"If only there was something I could do to help," Lupe wailed, wiping her eyes with her apron.

"Well, you are doing something, Lupe. You're keeping the house going and meals cooked and everything around here running. I know Reid really appreciates that. It's very important."

"You're very kind, Señorita Loren," Lupe murmured. "Very nice to let me cry and make me feel good about doing nothing."

"Lupe, personally I'm very glad you're here. You're keeping me company. I would be very lonely without you here in this big, rambling house."

"Some company," Lupe sniffed.

"You've been marvelous. Now, tell me what in the world you're cooking. It smells wonderful!" Loren peeked into the pot that was simmering on the stove. She listened attentively as Lupe explained her method of making Reid's favorite *salsa*.

Around noon Reid returned. He explained to a very

123

worried Lupe that his father was in stable condition and doing well.

"Lupe, 'stable' means he isn't getting worse. Not now, anyway. They are giving him medicine to fight the infections. You know he's a strong man. He'll pull through this." He placed a reassuring arm around her rounded shoulders and hugged her.

"Is he awake?" Loren asked.

"Yes." Reid smiled grimly. "And he recognized me. Gave me hell for loafing around the hospital. Said I should get to work!"

Lupe smiled, somewhat relieved with the tale. "Oh, Señor Reid, I'm so happy. My prayers have been answered!" She crossed herself quickly.

Reid held his hands up. "I'm not saying there is no more danger, but things are looking up. Now, this man's hungry, Lupe. Could we have some of your terrific soft tacos? I've missed them terribly. You'll never guess what this lady tried to feed me not two days ago!"

"What, Señor Reid?" Lupe's eyes grew large.

Reid shook his head. "Oh, I don't dare tell you, Lupe! It would ruin your meals for the next week!"

"No!" She cast a questioning look at Loren, then back to Reid's scowling face. "What is it, Señor Reid?"

"It wouldn't be fair, Lupe." He sighed. "Well, maybe . . ."

She leaned toward him curiously. "Yes?"

He whispered loudly. "A creature from the sea, Lupe! With crawly legs and big eyes!"

"No! No! I don't want to hear more!" She covered her ears. "I'll fix the tacos! Not another word!" Lupe made a dash for the door while Reid chuckled devilishly.

"Loren needs some lessons on how to cook real food,

124

Lupe! Will you help her?" He called laughingly after the retreating woman.

"*Sí, sí,* Señor Reid!" Lupe's voice trailed off as she escaped his taunting.

The mood had switched from one of mourning to a lighter one. Reid's very presence did it. He managed to give everyone a sense of security and a feeling that everything would be all right. Yes, Reid was home. *Home . . .*

Loren gazed over the strange landscape. Would she ever look at it and not think, *How strange?*

"You're good for her, Reid. She has been extremely worried about your father. A little diversion and a few laughs were exactly what she needed."

Reid ran his hand wearily through his hair. "I know this has been a heavy load for her to handle. I'm sure she feels somewhat responsible for being essentially in charge of the hacienda when he got sick. But it just couldn't be helped. She must realize that she isn't to blame."

"Well, you certainly gave her some relief. And I'm glad Senator Mecena is better, Reid."

He raised his eyebrows. "He's still in serious condition, Loren."

"Then why—"

"I didn't really lie about his condition, just stretched it somewhat. His life signs are now stable. That, in itself, is hopeful. But he's still struggling to live. Problem is, Raul took my father to the hospital and stayed with him until I arrived. Of course, Dad has tubes everywhere and oxygen and the heart monitor beeping all the time. All that just scared the hell out of Raul, and he spread his fears to everyone around here. So I've got to keep their spirits up, with false hope if necessary, so they can continue their work. My father needs them to continue their work. So do

I. Dad would really raise hell if he knew they were sitting around, wringing their hands."

Loren smiled at his comments, recalling Lupe's almost exact words. "Somehow I think they all know that!"

Reid began unbuttoning his western shirt. "Let's take a quick swim before lunch. That pool looks so inviting to me, and I can't think of a better way to enjoy it than with you."

"Okay, it's a deal. Meet you in a minute!" Loren agreed, hurrying to follow Reid in the house.

As she slid the shimmery green swimsuit up her long, straight legs and over slender hips, Loren reflected on how wonderful it was to have the liberty to swim and relax in this desert world of Reid's. It gave her the opportunity to unwind with no commitments, no appointments, no noisy traffic. It was wonderful! She hadn't realized just how much she had needed this little vacation, marred though it was by Reid's father's illness.

What an adjustment Reid had made-when he first came to Washington and adopted her very city-oriented way of life. Except for the cowboy boots, he had blended well. At least enough for her to fall in love with him . . . and hold on to that love for six cheerless years. Now that he was back in her life, she intended to enjoy every treasured moment.

Loren arrived on the veranda in time to see Reid, clad in a brief black bikini, stretch to his full masculine length. With an easy spring of taut leg muscles, he dove into the blue-green water, making barely a splash. She took a shaky breath, blatantly admiring the athletic form of this man whom she had loved for so long. His dark head emerged, and he swam the entire length of the pool with long, smooth strokes.

Loren stood by the pool's edge until Reid motioned her

in. The hot Arizona sun warmed her shoulders and the sight of Reid's appealing virility radiated feminine cravings throughout her body. She dove into the cold water, and the fire within her cooled quickly. She came to the surface with a healthy shout and was immediately engulfed in Reid's arms, pulling her to his scantily clad body.

"Dios mío! You are gorgeous in that suit, woman! Is this really my Loren?" Laughingly he ran his large masculine hands down her slick form, pausing to cup her breasts and tease the nipples, then stroke ever downward over ribs and around her slim waist. When his hands reached her hips, they caressed the slight curve, relishing her femininity, then pressed her to him.

Loren floated against him, instinctively wrapping her long legs around him to stay above water. She felt his passion-aroused force against her groin as his hands dug into the flesh of her buttocks. She reached for his shoulders and, with a teasing shriek, pushed his head under water and swam away from his roving hands.

"Hey!" he shouted upon emerging from the shimmery depths. "You'll pay for that, woman!" And he swam playfully after her.

She giggled as he pulled her against him again, this time sealing her mouth with his. Breathlessly she clung to him, drinking of his intoxicating kiss, allowing their passion to mingle. His lips were persistent, his tongue quickly penetrating to taste her sweetness. She met his probing with a welcoming of her own and shamelessly clamped her legs around his waist as the two of them floated to a warm haven far beyond the blazing Arizona sun. While Reid's lips incited her wanton abandon, his hands moved underwater and under her suit to excite her intimately.

The touch of her breasts, cold against his palms, tore at his control. When those dark peaks stood up to his satisfaction, he stroked elsewhere—downward over her slick-suited hips. Sensuously running long, curious fingers around the legs of her suit, he found easy access to further probing, adding to her eagerness by the minute.

Suddenly a noise attracted Loren beyond her desire-crazed state, and she looked up to see Lupe making her way down the steps and toward the pool with a tray laden with food. "Reid, it's Lupe!" she muttered against his lips. Reluctantly the two of them broke free from each other and swam apart underwater.

Reid emerged near the pool's edge and cast a winning one-dimpled smile at Lupe. "Hi! What have you got there, Lupe? Did you bring beer?"

"Sí, Señor Reid." Lupe nodded, not looking him in the eye. "I just thought you and Señorita Loren would like lunch by the pool."

"As usual, Lupe, that's a great idea!" Reid boomed. "We'd love it! What would I do without you?"

She cast him a faithful look, appeased by his enthusiastic praise. "There have been several calls this morning. I said you would return them after lunch. Is that all right?"

"Yes, that's fine, Lupe. Thanks." He pushed his muscular body easily out of the water, then turned to watch Loren's slender form climb the ladder.

"Thank you, Lupe." Loren smiled. "It looks wonderful!"

Lupe set the tray on the umbrella table and walked away, a small, satisfied smile tugging her lips.

"You are so luscious in that suit, I don't know if I can eat my lunch with you so tantalizing across the table!" Reid affirmed.

"Brrr! You don't have to worry! I freeze the minute this dry air hits me, so I'll just slip on this robe!" Loren grabbed the thick terry-cloth wrap. "How can I be so cold when it's so dang hot out here?"

He followed her to the table. "The water evaporates from your skin so rapidly because of the low humidity. That's what chills you. But you'll warm up soon enough, when you try Lupe's *burro*."

Loren glanced down at the plateful of food. "I thought you said tacos. What's this?"

"This, my Anglo *señorita,* is a *burro.* It's spicy meat, called chorizo, wrapped in a flour tortilla. Lupe calls it a soft taco, and nobody makes them as good as she does! You'll love them. Here's the sauce."

Her eyes traveled from the red to the green *salsa,* each full of interesting-looking ingredients. "Which is the hot one?"

He looked up and smiled. "You'd better try the green *salsa* until you get used to our food."

She spooned the thick sauce over the cheese-covered *burro* and sampled a bite.

"Well, how is it?" He waited anxiously.

"This isn't the hot one?" she gasped, grabbing for a beer.

"Nope." He grinned, generously spooning red *salsa* on his food. "Delicious, isn't it?"

"Once you get past the burning, it does have a nice flavor," Loren admitted timidly.

"Same could be said for a lot of things, *mi amor* !" Reid laughed.

Loren gave him a menacing look and ignored his comment. "This place is different in all ways. Even the food is strange."

Reid leaned over his plate. "Strange? You, who ate that . . . that damned scraggly animal on a sandwich, have the gall to call this food strange?"

"Speaking of strange animals," she smiled sweetly. "I was enchanted this morning by the local wildlife. On the way to the stables I scared a jackrabbit with those giant ears. And a roadrunner was as close to me as the pool! He twisted his head all the way around and glared at me. Then those cute little quail marched by and scattered under the cactus."

"You've had a good initiation, but there are more. We also have coyotes, coatimundi, and bighorn sheep in the mountains. How would you like to go horseback riding in the Catalinas tomorrow?"

"I'd love it! Could we?"

"Sure. I'll get my business under control this afternoon and leave tomorrow free. Depends, of course, on how Dad is. But we'll plan on it, okay?" His contented gaze settled on her, happy to have her close, in his world.

After lunch Reid spent several hours in his office, then headed downtown for meetings and another trip to the hospital.

Loren was left to her own devices. She lounged in the sun as long as she dared, then ambled inside where the coolness invited her to take a brief nap. She spent a heavenly hour in the Jacuzzi, her mind roaming to the limits of her imagination. As the turbulent water rushed around her legs and churned over her back and breasts, she thought of Reid. How exciting it would be to have him there with her! She leaned back and closed her eyes, dreaming about his body pressed urgently against her. It probably wouldn't take much persuasion to convince him to join her! She made a mental note of that!

By evening, when Reid returned, they were both hungry for each other. One starved exchange of glances between them and it was obvious. He was weary and the sight of

Loren's blue-violet eyes and relaxed smile made him ever grateful he had persuaded her to come along.

Loren thought there was a definite slump in the squareness of Reid's shoulders tonight. Perhaps it was the heavy load he was carrying, plus the unfinished business of the water bill in Washington.

"Wine?" he asked, opening the tall liquor cabinet.

"Sure," she nodded.

He poured, handed her a glass, then carried the bottle with him. "Come on. This is the prettiest part of the day. Out here, *mi amor.*"

They sipped dry wine on the veranda while the setting sun sent its magnificent explosion of color across the western sky. They spoke very little—just enjoyed.

Lupe approached the quiet couple on the porch. "Everything's done, Señor Reid. Your dinner is in the warming oven."

Fine, Lupe. We'll see you in the morning."

"Buenas noches, Señor Reid, Señorita Loren."

Loren smiled at her new friend. "Good evening, Lupe. Thanks for making me feel so much at home here."

"Sí, señorita."

"Good night, Lupe." Reid waved her away. "Go on and take care of your family. And thanks for everything."

"Where does she live, Reid?" Loren asked as Lupe's car drove away.

"She has a small place in the barrio. Remarkable woman. She has two children of her own and is keeping the teenaged son of her sister, who died last year. A few years ago that bastard she married deserted them, leaving her with two small children to support."

"She seems to be a wonderful employee. Very loyal."

"Oh, she's terrific. Like part of the family. We tried to

131

persuade her to move out here, but she keeps hoping her husband will return to the family someday."

"Well, she's extremely grateful to you and your father, believe me. Why, she thinks the sun rises and sets with your dad . . . and with you!" Loren boasted.

"What about you, Loren?"

She laughed and scoffed. "I know better, *Señor* Reid!"

"Do you know that I need you?" His voice was low and serious.

"I'm glad I came, Reid. I can see you're under stress." Her hand touched his arm.

"Can you see that I want you . . . now? Now, Loren." Reid's dark eyes were sable signals of suppressed passion that beckoned to her.

Loren's eyes inadvertently traveled down Reid's lengthy frame as he sat lounging in the casual chair beside her. His fingers trapped the delicate wineglass at his waist. One thumb rubbed the glass impatiently. Below his flat waist his slacks pulled tautly, revealing the masculine burgeoning where his legs met.

God! He was appealing and virile and, to Loren, irresistible.

"Reid?" She grinned mischievously as her eyes rose to meet his. "Before dinner?"

"Why not?"

She shrugged, submission quivering on the ends of her every nerve.

He stood and pulled her up against him. "I can give you fifty good reasons not to wait. Mainly, though, I want you . . . want to love you, Loren." His kiss was a torch that lit passionate embers within them both, kindling explosive tinder. Flames of desire shot through her limbs, and she opened her lips to his probing tongue.

The flavor of wine lingered, and Loren relished the taste

of him, the heady fragrance of his skin. Reid's soft mustache tantalizingly brushed her intoxicated lips, the exquisite column of her neck, the noble curve of her breasts. His kiss, his touch, sent whorls of desire spiraling drunkenly through her veins, and she writhed with undisguised pleasure.

Breathless and giddy, Loren leaned against him, locking her arms around his neck. Wildly she wanted to press him into every cell, every inch of her. She never wanted to forget the resilience of his solid chest and the flourish of his taut maleness, aroused so urgently by her touch.

Her hands roamed recklessly down his chest to free his shirt from the belted slacks. Exploring fingers moved under his shirt, caressing his bare ribs, traveling his spine, surveying his lower back. Her slender fingers dug into his firm buttocks and, instinctively, Reid thrust his hips ardently against hers.

She shifted away slightly to allow one brazen hand to slide around and cup his groin. With affirmed satisfaction Loren knew that Reid was within the power of her touch. Curious hands continued their ecstatic torment until, with a distressed groan, Reid swept her up in his arms.

Forgotten were their wineglasses, their waiting dinner, even the illness that brought them to Arizona. Loren was aware only of being carried to heaven and the fiery trail of Reid's lips on her neck and half-exposed breasts. By the time they reached his bedroom, she was burning with an inner fever that could be quenched only by Reid's matching passion.

"Reid! Be careful!" She gasped as he tore vigorously at her sundress.

"Careful?" he growled. "After what you did to me out on the veranda? You're lucky I didn't lay you down on that cold Mexican tile!"

With quick, shaky hands Loren discarded the flimsy dress. "You don't want to cool things too much, do you?" she taunted.

He reached for her. "With this heat between us, I'm not worried, *mi amor!*" His lips played over her tight, aching breasts, then encased each alert nipple.

With a delicate moan she began unbuttoning Reid's shirt. She could only think of his proud, magnificent body loving her, relieving the burning fever in them both. While he swiftly shucked his remaining clothes, Loren's hands raked over his body, examining and inflaming.

"Por Dios, woman! You're driving me crazy!"

"Good," she murmured as she kissed the cords in his neck. "I've been crazy since you entered my life!"

"We must belong together then." He paused before her, his eyes drinking in the sight of her nude form.

"We do," she agreed, permitting him careful scrutiny of her silken figure. His dark eyes devoured her, creating a savage yearning in her loins.

With deliberate slowness, he molded his masculine contours to her feminine counterparts, pressing hairy thighs to her smooth ones, his muscular, flat belly to her softer flesh, his unyielding chest crushing her pliable breasts. Within moments they were stretched across the big bed together.

His hand traveled familiar paths, gently teasing the most sensitive parts of her body. Loren gasped with delight as he stroked her stomach and inner thighs.

"Don't stop—"

"I must. Come to me . . ." He pulled her over him, continuing his sensuous persuasion.

Eagerly, responsively, Loren settled him deeply inside her. She arched to meet his abundant masculinity, utilizing the skills he had taught her for both their ultimate pleasure. Together they reached a frenetic, wild zenith, each grasping for more of the other. They were as one, belonging and cherishing, their wild hunger at last being satisfied.

Finally Loren relaxed her heaving breasts on his chest. She nibbled the side of his neck where her face lay. The descent from the heights was a slow, wonderful journey, interspersed by an occasional warm kiss or murmur of love.

"Loren, *mi amor,* you're amazing." Reid's voice was muffled against her temple.

"Your love is wonderful." She smiled contentedly and kissed his still-throbbing neck.

"I can never get enough of you, Loren," he sighed, rolling her into the cradle of his arm.

"Never?" A teasing finger traced his hipline. "What about now . . . again?"

"Later, my sexy *señorita*" He laughed from deep within his chest. "First, the Jacuzzi . . . together. Next, dinner. Your man's hungry! Then . . ." He smiled wickedly. "Then, *mi preciosa,* whatever you want!"

"Promise?" She tweaked a dark hair.

"Promise!"

CHAPTER EIGHT

Loren's eyelids fluttered with the sudden intrusion of light across her face.

"Wake up, sleepyhead," a low masculine voice muttered. "Do you think you're going to sleep all day? We have mountains to climb!"

"Hmmm . . . what mountains?"

"You do want to climb the Catalinas, don't you? Why, we might even find gold in them thar hills!"

"Who cares?" She turned over and covered her head with the pillow.

"Come on, *mi amor.* Lupe has a mountaineer's breakfast on the table, and lunch packed in the saddlebags. We need to get an early start before the heat of the day and the monsoons roll in!" He swatted her firmly on the rump and opened the shutters to admit the sun.

"Why didn't you remind me last night that we'd be getting up with the sun?" she groaned.

"Oh, no!" he chuckled. "My thoughts were elsewhere last night! Breakfast is waiting. You don't want to miss this opportunity to ride into the mountains searching for gold, do you? Think of all the exciting tales you can take back to your dull friends in Washington!" He closed the door, leaving her to dress alone.

When Loren finally stumbled into the kitchen, Lupe

greeted her with a wide smile. *"Buenos días, señorita! Coffee?"*

"Oh, yes!"

"Señor Reid wants to have breakfast on the veranda."

"Thank you, Lupe."

At Reid's urging, Loren ate more than usual for breakfast. Maybe it was the cool, fresh Arizona air that increased her appetite. Or maybe it was the marvelous variety of fresh fruit and delicious breads prepared by Lupe. At any rate, she was only too glad to follow Reid's lead and wolf down their feast. Within the hour they were loaded with lunch, plenty of water, and high spirits for riding into the Catalinas.

"We'll see you sometime this afternoon, Lupe," Reid advised. Then, placing a reassuring hand on her shoulder, he added, "I talked with the doctor this morning. Dad had a restful night and seems to be improving. So don't worry about him."

"Sí, Señor Reid." Lupe nodded obediently. "Be careful. Don't forget, Señorita Loren is a gringo!"

"I know," he chuckled. "We'll be back before the monsoons have a chance to blow in."

"Please be careful of the *chubasco!"* Lupe motioned overhead at the usually solid blue sky. "We already have clouds!"

"Don't worry, Lupe." He helped Loren mount her horse.

A misty haze settled over the Catalinas as they rode up the rocky path into the cactus-covered heights. They rose rapidly above the hacienda and stopped long enough to view the stretch of Oro Valley and the far Tucson Mountains with their pinkish glow.

"This is just beautiful, Reid. Now, what monsoon were

you and Lupe discussing?" Loren encouraged her horse beside Reid's so they could talk.

"Oh, for several months in the summer we have what everyone calls the monsoon season. Lupe calls it *chubasco,* which means sudden thunderstorm. That more aptly describes it. It's our rainy season."

"Rain? Out here? Looks like you haven't had rain in months."

"Well, it doesn't rain in the same spot every day. Sometimes the clouds sail right over us. Now, for the last couple of days, you could see the rain falling in the Sonoran Desert. But when it does rain, watch out. It comes hard and fast, creating flash floods and bringing intense electricity."

"Oh." Loren nodded, not really understanding the full impact of what he was saying. To her, rain was rain. It fell frequently in Washington, and it was no big deal.

"As we go farther into the mountains, keep your eyes and ears open for the bighorn sheep."

"I thought bighorn sheep were all in the Rockies or Alaska!"

"No. There's a small herd along this Pusche Ridge Area. They're protected as endangered species and are very elusive. Our chance of sighting them will increase at higher elevations."

Loren noticed that the seemingly barren, lifeless desert was alive with activity. Their horses startled numerous cottontail and jackrabbits while an occasional brazen chipmunk would scurry across their path.

By noon they had traveled to another ecological zone. Plant growth consisted not only of numerous types of cacti, but of various medium-size trees that provided shade. Reid even found a small trickle of a stream, allowing a brief cool respite from the increasing heat of the

Arizona sun. Loren again ate as if it were her last meal, savoring the spicy meat on her sandwich. Maybe she was acquiring a taste for the snappy Mexican food, because she thought it was delicious.

She stretched her legs and walked around the small, shaded harbor. "What kind of tree is this, Reid? Its trunk is green and leaves look like tiny lace."

"Palo Verde tree," he answered. "That's chlorophyll in their bark. Gets them through the dry seasons."

"And those fuzzy-looking cacti?"

"Oh, they aren't fuzzy! They're vicious!" he chuckled. "That's a cholla, pronounced *cho-ya*. It's also called a jumping cactus because if you brush against it, little chunks of it break off and cling to you!"

"There are so many different kinds of cacti out here, Reid. I always thought they were all alike."

"No, not at all. You know, there are some plants that grow here and nowhere else on earth. Those giant saguaro, for instance."

She glanced curiously at the tall, spiny plants. "They look like a cowboy being held up with a gun in his back," she mused. "See, his arms are up."

"It takes a hundred years for it to grow one branch, or arm, as you call it."

"A hundred years?" she asked incredulously. "Then most of these were around when the Indians roamed this land."

He nodded with a grin. "The Spaniards, the Indians, the miners—all of them!"

"The miners? Did you say earlier there's gold up here?"

"Oh, sure. Somewhere."

"These aren't the famous Superstition Mountains, are they?"

"Oh, no. The Superstitions are farther to the north. But

the Catalinas have their own tales of gold too. Many a man spent his life—and lost it—searching for gold up here."

Loren's eyes narrowed as she tried to imagine such a life. "It's amazing."

"They say there's still a mine, hidden by time and rocks, that the Jesuit priests used in the seventeenth century. Supposedly they locked it up with an iron door so no one could get to the gold. *La mina con la puerta de hierro en la Cañada del Oro.*"

"Oh, Reid, how exciting! Wouldn't it be an experience to search for it?" Her face was alight with the prospect.

"No! My God, Loren! People have been searching for that thing for years and nobody's found more than a few trickles of placer gold! I doubt that there's even a lode up here!"

"Oh, Reid, where's your sense of adventure?" She took his hand and squeezed it.

He kissed her nose. "My sense of adventure wants to guide us to a special field of wild flowers where we might spot those bighorn sheep, then back down off this treacherous mountain before these clouds build up any higher."

"Spoilsport!" Loren fussed as she mounted her horse and followed Reid up the ever-narrowing trail that led through a dry wash.

They found the field, but not the bighorn sheep. Reid was clearly disappointed, but Loren was far more interested in the possibility of gold. She began to look at every granite boulder and pile of sandstone rock with renewed interest.

However, Reid was intent on the growing dark clouds that blocked the burning sun. Shadows spotted the terrain, and instead of stopping by the stream on their return, they shared a drink from Reid's canteen and kept moving. Suddenly the air was cool and a moist breeze buffeted them from the south. The sky darkened and the temperature dropped noticeably. Reid urged Loren to hurry. As he had suspected, the rains came before they made it home. After trying to continue for a short distance in the cold rain, he finally decided they should take refuge somewhere.

The desert storm became violent quickly, with loud cracking of thunder and brilliant streaks of lightning stretching from black, menacing sky to brown, drenched earth. It was spectacular, but there was no time to enjoy the beauty. Loren wrestled to control her horse, but lost her seat when he bolted wildly.

Reid lunged at the bridle, but the animal reared frantically and broke away down the obscure mountain trail. He turned his attention to Loren, who was huddling in a muddy heap. Dismounting, he quickly tied his horse to a sturdy scrub oak and gathered her in his arms.

"Hey, baby, are you all right?"

"Depends on what you call all right!" she snapped. "I'm cold, wet, muddy, and humiliated! Otherwise I'm fine!"

"No broken bones? Then come on!" Roughly he pulled her to her feet, and they scrambled across a stretch of sodden sandstone until they reached a ledge of limestone. "Under here," he commanded.

The limestone ledge provided limited protection from the rain, although tiny rivulets crept inward to where Reid and Loren huddled. The sudden drop in temperature left its chilling effect.

Loren clung to Reid, seeking a warmth he couldn't provide. "I'm so miserable! This place is awful! Let's get out of here."

He cradled her to his wet shirt. "I know, baby. But we can't leave yet. We're safe under here." His dark eyes watched the transformation of the dry washes to treacherous riverbeds of rushing water. Above them he could hear the crashing of a wall of water in the area they had just traversed. Within minutes that wall rushed past them, clearing out everything in its path. He could only hope that Loren's horse was well out of the way by now. And that his remained tied.

Even after the rain had halted they had to remain in place, waiting for the heavy runoff to subside. There was no leaving their small limestone refuge until the way they must travel was safe. So they lingered, cold and miserable.

Several bone-chilling hours later Reid stirred. "I think we can start to make our way back now. We may have to walk part of the way."

Loren was so cold, she was shaking all over. She moved woodenly, but followed him, knowing there was no other way out. They led Reid's horse as they hiked down the steepest part. Stumbling over the sodden earth, Loren was grateful for her heavy cowboy boots. It didn't matter that mud was caked two inches thick all over them. Thankfully the cacti she brushed against didn't penetrate the heavy leather. She hoped fervently that this was the last time she would ever need those damned boots!

Finally they reached an area where the horse could retain his footing. Reid heaved himself into the saddle and pulled Loren snuggly behind him. She clung limply to his broad, wet back, wishing the time would fly, and they could be home immediately.

"Look, Loren, a rainbow over the Tucsons! Bet you don't often see one that stretches from horizon to horizon."

She looked at the 180-degree arc of colors over the distant mountains and admitted to herself that it was gorgeous. However, she was in no mood to expound on the

142

beauties of the desert and mumbled a barely audible, "Yeah."

"And that refreshing smell after a rain!" Reid heaved a deep breath, inhaling the air satisfyingly. "You don't get that in the city, Loren."

"You're right. I have never gotten this in the city!" she grated.

"The creosote bush has a special fragrance when it gets wet," he explained.

"Strange, strange place," Loren muttered.

They rode on quietly, two wet, cold people silhouetted against a picturesque pink and orange sunset. At dusk they were received by welcoming hands and the worried prattle of Lupe.

She motioned in the air, angry, yet relieved. "I told you! *El chubasco!* When that horse came back, I knew. I just knew! *Ayy, Dios mío! Gracias a Dios!*" She crossed herself, then continued fussing and gesturing.

Reid interrupted her with tired directives. "Sorry we worried you, Lupe. Would you take care of Loren while I help Raul with the horses and saddles?"

"*Sí, claro.* Of course. Come with me, *pobrecita.*" Lupe draped Loren's shoulders with a colorful Mexican shawl and helped her discard the leaden boots, then, murmuring words of comfort, led her inside.

While Loren stripped off her cold, wet blouse and jeans, Lupe ran hot water in the tub. Gratefully Loren sank into the warm liquid, allowing it to cover her, hoping its warmth would seep into her chilled bones.

By the time she could hear Reid running the shower next door, she was snuggly tucked into bed, sipping hot tea laced with something. But Loren was so tired, she didn't even bother to ask Lupe what it was. There was a

143

cup of marvelous soup, which Loren drank quickly, then slumped down in the big bed . . . alone.

What a day this had been! The land had changed so quickly—had actually turned on them! It became their enemy, trying in every way to drive them away, or destroy them. What had started out to be a hot summer day ended up cold and harsh. What began as an adventure for her and Reid resulted in disaster. It was no wonder miners lost their lives hunting the elusive gold! One rainstorm and they were all swept away! How frightening!

Loren drifted off to sleep with visions of herself and Reid riding mules into the mountains on an ill-fated search for gold.

CHAPTER NINE

It wasn't the sunlight that woke her. The room had a grayish tint instead of its usual sunny yellow. One glance at the bedside clock told Loren that she had slept over twelve hours. She lay very still, enjoying her relaxed state, the warmth that permeated her chilled body, the marvelous aroma coming from somewhere else in the hacienda. Maybe that's what had awakened her, she mused as her stomach growled.

With muscle-aching effort, she rolled out of bed, wrapped herself in her blanket, and opened the shutters to look outside. The Catalina Mountains loomed innocently as low clouds settled around them like plugs of cotton. They appeared innocuous, incapable of abrupt danger. But Loren knew better.

A soft knock at her door was followed by a gentle "Señorita Loren? Are you awake?"

"Yes, Lupe. Come on in." She turned away from the window.

"Oh, Señorita Loren, Señor Reid has a surprise for you!" And she slipped back out the door.

Oh, no, not another one! Loren groaned inwardly and pulled the blanket tighter around her flimsy nightgown.

Within another minute Reid was entering the room, clutching a huge tray laden with food and a tall green

145

bottle. He was dressed in casual brown slacks and a dark tan open-collared shirt, which served only to provide a devastating framework for his black hair and eyes. His skin was as tanned as the shirt, giving him the appearance of being shirtless. Loren looked away, telling herself that his masculine appearance didn't affect her. *As if that were possible!*

Setting the tray on the bedside table, Reid poured the bubbly liquid into two glasses. He walked over to Loren and stood close. Unable to avert her eyes completely, Loren watched his chest rise and fall behind the glasses. He placed one delicate crystal in her hand. *"Salud, mi amor."*

She raised her eyes to his dark ones and chafed, "To my health? We're lucky to be alive! We should be toasting the fact that we're not at the bottom of some dry gulch somewhere in Cañada del Oro!"

Reid's dark eyes flickered with ire, but he managed to retain a cool exterior. Tilting the sparkling glass toward her, he acquiesced. "To our lives, then." He made the effort to click his glass to hers, then gulped half the contents. Wheeling sharply away, he ordered, "Have some breakfast, Loren. We have a full day ahead if you want to travel to Bisbee and visit with Emmaline Walker. It'll take about two hours to get there." The warm spark was gone from his tone. Loren had doused those embers.

She walked toward him, dragging half the wide-striped Mexican blanket behind her while clutching the other end around bare shoulders. "Yes, I do want to see Emmaline today. I was just . . . checking the weather."

His answer was curt. "It won't matter today, Loren. We'll go in the four-wheel-drive truck."

"It looks like rain."

146

"The cloud-cover will help hold the temperature down. Rain never bothered you before."

"My life has never been threatened by it before."

If she was waiting for apologies from this arrogant man, Loren could tell that she would have to wait all day . . . and then some!

"That's the way it is out here, Loren. Sometimes survival is a challenge. When my great-grandfather came out here and settled, survival was a way of life, not only from the weather. Indians were a major threat. That's a part of my heritage." Reid shoved a bowl of fruit into her hands, then took his breakfast and settled in the rugged rawhide chair near the window. His ebony eyes raked over her, leaving a chill like the rain of the previous day.

Loren sat on the bed and turned to her bowl of fruit like a sulking child. Finally she offered hesitantly, "Thank you for the champagne breakfast. I'm sorry if I've spoiled it."

"I guess it was spoiled before it began."

Loren sipped her champagne thoughtfully. *What a rotten way to start the day!* "Reid, I can't help it if I think this desert is strange. It's alien to everything I know, everything I'm familiar with."

He smiled grimly. "I'll admit it's vastly different from Washington, D.C."

"In a million ways," she answered softly.

"Yes, I suppose so," he agreed with a sigh.

"Coffee, anyone?" Lupe's smiling face and warm cheerfulness entered the overcast room along with the most aromatic coffee Loren had ever inhaled.

"Oh, yes," she answered quickly. "Champagne for breakfast is not my usual fare. I think I'll need some coffee before I go anywhere today."

"Me too." Reid rose and lumbered over to fill the western-size coffee mugs, lacing each with thick, rich cream.

"How's your father?" Loren blurted out. With a pang of conscience she realized that she hadn't even thought of the hospitalized man in over twenty-four hours. Her only concern had been their experience on the mountain. She hadn't even thought of him when she was home, warm and safe in bed . . . in *his* home!

Before Reid could reply, Lupe broke in spiritedly, "Oh, he's much better! He called me this morning with instructions to send the ledger in to the hospital when Reid comes! That means he's getting well!"

"The ledger? You mean he wants to work? Are you going to let him do that, Reid?" Loren questioned.

Reid's face was tight, but there was a degree of restrained relief evident in his eyes. "Oh, he's not in any shape to work, although he thinks he is. But it's a good sign, as Lupe says."

"Oh, Reid and Lupe, I'm so glad the senator is better. I know you both have been so worried about him."

Lupe smiled and murmured, *"Sí, gracias,* Señorita Loren. Enjoy your breakfast." She left the elaborate silver coffee urn on the table.

"Seems funny to be relieved when Dad's sitting up in bed raising hell." Reid smiled. "But that's just the way he is."

"Reid, I feel so guilty. I didn't even think about him last night. Did you—"

"Go to the hospital? Yes, *mi amor.* After you were warm and asleep in *my* bed, I drove downtown to check on Dad."

"Oh, Reid." Loren's eyes were large and sorrowful when Reid crossed the room to her. Cupping her face in his dark hands, he stared deeply into her blue eyes for a long minute. That overpowering gaze, his electric touch, the masculine fragrance of the man commanding her femi-

148

nine response, came together in a heart-pounding cacophony inside her.

In a totally reflexive action her hands reached up to cover his, and the energy that flowed between them as they touched was detectable in a powerful, almost tangible way. A wellspring of jubilance swelled inside Loren as Reid looked at her.

Eventually even the towering self-control Reid exhibited crumbled and his lips caught hers in a clasp of emotional fervor. The kiss was long and spoke candidly of his desire for her. His tongue edged her lips, then sought the recesses of her sweet mouth until the combination of love and longing cast a spell of absorbing unity between them.

Somewhere, sometime, Loren was drawn and lifted to Reid, this man she loved . . . had loved for years. Their spirits combined in that one kiss so infinitely that they both knew its full implications.

"Oh, God, Loren—" he rasped when he finally lifted his head.

"What . . . what do you want from me?"

"Your love is all I ask." His voice was low and hoarse. "I don't give a damn what you think of Arizona or the desert or the mountains. The only thing I care about is what you feel for me. And I think that was answered just now, Loren. You can't hide your feelings from me, *mi amor.* Don't deny your love again."

He broke the electric trance and strode across the room, leaving Loren to stare after him, dazed and confused.

Then he turned to her and ordered in a surprisingly tame tone, "Be ready to go to Bisbee in an hour. I'll be back from the hospital then." He closed the large wooden door behind him while Loren sat wrapped in the brightly colored Mexican blanket. She sipped her champagne and wrestled with her emotions alone.

149

A short hour ago, when she had awakened, Loren thought that she hated everything about this strange desert land, including Reid Mecena. Mostly she hated him for what happened yesterday. They had been in physical danger and it was his fault! The ride into the mountains had been his idea. The day and direction had been his. She had gone along in innocence. It had sounded like fun. Good, safe fun.

Never mind that she had looked forward to the activity with enthusiasm. *He* was at fault here. *Reid!* Or was she blaming him because she wanted to relieve herself? Because she sought an excuse to find fault with the man she loved . . . and therefore reason to end their relationship?

Oh, dear God! She buried her hands in her face. It had been like this when she had been pregnant, then miscarried. In her numbed mind Reid was responsible for all that grief and unhappiness. She had overlooked her own role in the pregnancy, simply because she wanted to have a reason to blame him. To hate him. But could she? Could she hate him now? He claimed not. Could he tell from one kiss? One breathtaking, all-encompassing kiss?

Loren walked to the window. What did she want? Did she want to love him . . . or hate him? Did she actually have that choice?

Before they left for Bisbee, Loren called the family of Emmaline Walker to announce their impending visit. They made the trip in relative silence, with Reid pointing out an occasional landmark. Loren was familiar enough with the Catalina Mountains to the north and the Tucsons, which framed the evening sunsets. The Rincons formed an eastern gateway leading to flat, uninteresting desert land bounded by towering, bare mountains in the distance. Geronimo country. With a little imagination Loren could visualize Geronimo on horseback, beckoning to thousands of his followers outlined against the gray sky. She almost expected to see an ominous half-naked figure rising behind every hill, decorated with war paint, and feathers fanned by the breeze.

"What are you thinking?" Reid broke the silence.

"You wouldn't believe it." She laughed spontaneously. "I was wondering if we would be ambushed by Indians over that next rise!"

"You must have spent many an hour chasing Indians on the screen with Gary Cooper and John Wayne!"

"Well, I'm in more of the *Gunsmoke* and *Tombstone Territory* era myself."

He chuckled. "What! No Hopalong Cassidy or Gene Autry or 'Hmmm, Kemo Sabe, what you think?' "

"Who's that?"

"Who was that masked man? Why, the Lone Ranger, of course! They were my heroes for years. And most of their movies were filmed right out here in Old Tucson. They still use the set occasionally."

She shook her head. "Filming in this heat is surely a test of your mettle as an actor." It sounded above and beyond the calling to her.

"Can you imagine living out here before the days of air-conditioning and deodorant?" Reid teased.

"I can't imagine living here at all!"

"My great-grandparents loved it. They came out for my great-grandfather's health. They fell in love with the wide-open spaces and strange desert creatures. His health improved so much that he could enjoy living again, and I suppose that had a lot to do with their love of the place." Although he responded calmly, there was a burning hurt underneath the surface.

"I suppose if you had a special reason . . ." Loren

reflected on the idea that some people lived here and loved it. It was a remote notion to her.

"Did you say you talked to Emmaline's family?" Reid asked.

"Yes. Her daughter. She was thrilled and said it would cheer her mother up to have us visit."

"Good. I imagine she'll be even more cheered when she finds out what you have to say about her long-delayed benefits!"

"Um-hum," Loren answered absently, observing the change of scenery as, having gained several thousand feet in altitude, they entered the picturesque mining town of Bisbee. Loren was first struck by the awesome sight of a gaping hole in the middle of town! They drove past the copper mine, located conveniently in the heart of the small city and the charming Victorian houses, complete with elaborate gingerbread eaves.

Reid stopped on the far outskirts of town before a roughhewn adobe and thatch house, which had long ago been bleached to a pale ecru by the Arizona sun. Loren took a deep breath, sad to see that her Navajo friend, the mother of a war hero, lived in such poverty. If she had only known, Loren would have fought for more than the son's minimal benefits! Loren had taken the easy route and accepted what was offered. Next time she would make other demands. *Next time . . . oh, yes!* She decided as she entered the modest abode, there will be a next time. *And I will go informed and demanding!*

"I'm so glad you came. Mother will be out in a few minutes." The dark-haired woman who opened the door greeted them. "I'm Silvie Tanner, Emmaline's daughter. This is my daughter, Tracy Lewis, and her new baby." She motioned proudly at the infant, who was sleeping peacefully in the arms of his mother.

"Please call me Loren," she said, then turned to introduce Reid.

As Silvie shook his hand, she repeated his name slowly. "Mecena . . . don't I know you?"

Reid nudged her memory. "You probably remember my father. He was a senator from Arizona a few years ago. Nice to meet you both."

"Oh, yes, I remember now. He spoke in Bisbee once. Please come in and have a seat."

The room was spartan but contained no lack of Indian art on the walls and stacked in corners. Weavings of all types, rugs, and pottery were abundant. There were even two looms pushed against the far wall, both containing half-finished items. Loren and Reid sat together on the hard, narrow couch.

Loren smiled at the young mother, a modern version of dark-skinned Navajo beauty. "May I see your baby?" she asked fondly.

"Certainly." Tracy eagerly shoved the warm bundle into Loren's arms. From that vantage point, both she and Reid hovered over the dark-haired infant.

"This is the first boy in our family in forty years," Silvie offered proudly. "We're very lucky to have this little one."

"You certainly are." Loren smiled when the baby stirred in his sleep. "He's a beautiful child. What's his name?"

"Ben," Tracy responded. "Benjamin Walker Lewis."

Loren's curious gaze met Silvie's dark eyes. "Benjamin Walker? After—"

Silvie nodded. "After my brother who died in the war. We convinced Mother it was the modern thing to do."

Reid looked uncomfortably at the baby and tentatively touched the tiny hand. "How old is he? He's so little."

153

"He's six weeks old now. That's why I couldn't accompany Mother to Washington. Tracy needed me."

Reid nodded, then tried to move his hand. But tiny Ben had grasped the large male finger and held on firmly while he slept contentedly. The women laughed softly at the expression on the captured Reid's face.

"I think he likes you, Reid. Here, would you like to hold him?" Loren suggested.

Reid's quick decline was congenial. "Not now, thanks. I . . . er, haven't washed my hands!" His expression was one of desperation as he tugged his finger away from the baby's tight grasp.

Emmaline Walker chose that moment to enter the room. "I see you have met my great-grandson. What do you think of him?" The pride of her ancestors glowed in Emmaline's dark eyes.

"Oh, Emmaline, he's just wonderful!" Loren handed the baby to his grandmother and rose to greet her friend. "I know you are proud of this baby. Of Ben."

Emmaline smiled up at Loren and spoke. "The child has a good name. We have placed much hope on this little one because he is male. Perhaps too much for such a tiny person. But that is the way. The men have the heavy burden these days. For forty years the women in this family have had it."

"I'm so glad you now have a boy." Loren smiled. "He will liven things up around here in a few years. You know, I have good news for you. I've talked with some people in Washington. You will be getting a check in the mail in a few weeks." Now, after seeing the conditions in which these women lived, Loren felt the sum a paltry amount. She was determined to fight for more.

"Oh, thank you, Loren!" Silvie exclaimed, suddenly overcome with tears of joy.

Emmaline's wrinkled countenance spread into a placid smile. "Oh, yes. I knew you would do it, Loren. You listened when no one else would."

"Actually it's what is rightfully yours, Emmaline. From Benjamin," Loren said modestly.

The old woman took a shaky breath. "See, my Benjamin is still taking care of us! Ah, that is too great a burden! Why can't we just let him die in peace?"

Silvie's voice was gentle. "We can, Mother. Now we will move back to Window Rock where we belong. There we can watch our baby Ben grow up in the land of his people."

"Yes." The old woman nodded slowly. "It is good."

Tracy broke the tight emotional spell. "How would everyone like some iced tea?"

"Yes, that sounds great," Reid eagerly agreed.

"I'll help you," Loren offered, and followed Tracy into the small kitchen. The windowpanes were of old, wavy glass and the refrigerator was almost of antique quality. "Are you anxious to move, Tracy?"

"Oh, yes," responded the young woman. "My husband, Paul, is working in Window Rock with a new Indian industry. And I want to take our baby there to live. Now, with this money, my mother and grandmother can move too. I can't tell you how much this means to us."

"You don't have to. I think I understand. Your family should be together." Loren ambled toward the crude shelf along the end wall holding rows of clay pots in various stages of completion. "Tell me about these, Tracy."

She shrugged. "That's Mother's pottery. She sells it whenever she has a chance. Aren't they nice?"

"Why, they're beautiful!" Loren began to examine some of the finished pottery. "Can Silvie continue to make her pottery and sell it in Window Rock?"

"Oh, yes. Through the Navajo Arts and Crafts Enterprise. They promote all things that Navajos make and provide a market. Here's your tea, Loren."

"Thank you. You know, I like this pottery so much, I want to take some back to Washington with me. Are these for sale?"

Tracy picked up the small plastic tray that held the tea glasses. "Sure!"

They joined the others in the midst of Silvie's animated explanation of the huge wooden loom in the corner of the room.

"Mother weaves the old Navajo way. Her rugs are very valuable, but it takes a long time to make them. Sometimes I help her when her eyes get tired. Here is a sample." She spread a smaller version of a Navajo rug weaving across her knees.

"Why, Mrs. Walker, your work is excellent. I think I could sell some of these rugs for you in Tucson," Reid proposed.

Emmaline rose slowly. "I have some rugs you can take with you today, Mr. Mecena."

"Fine! I'll have them sold by the end of the week, Mrs. Walker. I'm sure of it. Now, you must set the prices and advise me on quality and size. I definitely don't want them underpriced."

"I'll help you, Grandmother," Tracy said, and went with Emmaline to gather the rugs.

"I'd like to buy a couple of your pots, Silvie. They're beautiful," Loren said, and gestured to them.

"Thank you." Silvie smiled gratefully. "I just started making the pots a few years ago. I had always been a weaver, like my mother. Then a neighbor here in Bisbee, a Pueblo potter from New Mexico, taught me to work

156

with clay. My daughter gave me the encouragement to break with tradition. So now I do both."

"Well, I'm so glad Tracy urged you to branch out with your talents. What excellent artists you two are!"

"Did you see Tracy's weavings?" Silvie moved to expose the smaller loom. On it was an elaborate circular picture in free-flowing, woven pieces, depicting a western landscape in three-dimensional splendor. "Talk about breaking tradition! This girl has a mind of her own when it comes to weaving!"

"She certainly does!" agreed Loren, admiring the intricate designs.

"Now, Mother . . ." Tracy admonished as she laid an armful of Navajo rugs next to Reid.

"This is just beautiful, Tracy. Where did you learn to do this type of weaving? It's so different from what your mother and grandmother do," he commented.

Tracy smiled bashfully, obviously delighting in the praise she was receiving. "I had a good art teacher in high school who taught me various kinds of weaving, then set me free. I loved it. I'm sure my grandmother thinks I'm rebelling against tradition, but I only want to add to it."

"She is proud and happy when she sees what lovely weavings you make. She has seen a lot of change in her lifetime. Just look at the differences in life-styles since she was a young woman," Silvie reminded them.

Tracy nodded. "I know. I hope the Navajo life for my son will be different. I'm going to work to improve it."

"This woman has a good head on her shoulders, Silvie." Loren smiled her approval. "She is very talented and wise."

"As her mother, I have to agree with you." Silvie chuckled. "Why don't we choose those pots?"

Loren picked her favorite pots and Reid conferred with

157

Emmaline about the rugs. They loaded the truck in preparation for the journey back to Tucson.

Emmaline pressed a brilliant rug into Loren's arms, asserting with finality, "This is gift for you, Loren. You are woman who listens. I thank you."

Loren shook her head frantically. "Oh, no, I couldn't—"

"It won't do any good to try to change her mind," Silvie admonished. "She wants you to have it. We all do."

Loren looked helplessly at Reid. She felt extremely guilty, knowing how much these women needed money. The rug in her hands was worth around a thousand dollars. He gave her a barely discernible nod, and she smiled weakly. "Thank you, Emmaline. I will always treasure this gift from my Navajo friend. I hope we'll meet again." She hugged the old woman, then the other two in turn.

"Tracy, keep doing your unusual weavings and making your own traditions. Little Ben is just beautiful. You're very lucky.

"Silvie, thanks for everything. You have a wonderful family."

The women turned to go. Suddenly Loren gasped. "Silvie—" She scrambled in her purse. "Silvie, your mother didn't want this in Washington, and gave it to me. But I think you will value it. And so will little Ben, when he is old enough." She pressed the small box into Silvie's hand.

Silvie opened the lid to reveal the gleaming Silver Star awarded her brother, Benjamin Walker, for bravery in Saipan as a Navajo code talker. With tears overflowing her dark eyes, she nodded. "Yes, oh, yes. This is . . . beautiful. This is an honor we will cherish. I will save it for Ben. Thank you, Loren. Woman Who Listens. . . ."

"Explain to Emmaline why I can't keep it, please," Loren whispered through a growing lump in her own throat.

Silvie hugged her again and waved as they climbed into Reid's truck along with the load of valuable Navajo crafts.

They were silent for a while. Loren ran her hands over the firm weaving of Emmaline's rug. "Oh, Reid, those women need so much. It breaks my heart."

"You gave them exactly what they need, Loren. Encouragement and hope."

"But, I mean . . . so much more."

"I know. But they don't want anything given. No handouts. They're too proud. Look how long it took them to ask for the Marine benefits they deserve."

Loren glanced at Reid and one could almost see the wheels turning inside her head. "Reid, where is Window Rock? Would Raul mind driving a truckload of their furniture up there?"

Reid shrugged, considering the idea. "Window Rock is several hours north and east. It's in the Navajo reservation, near the New Mexico border."

"You know, I'll bet all of their household belongings would fit in the back of this pickup. The largest, most valuable items they have are the looms and finished crafts. Things would have to be packed very carefully, but they wouldn't take up much room." Her voice rose in pitch as her enthusiasm grew. "Now, you give me one good reason why Raul wouldn't want to make this trip. He could take another ranch hand along to assist in the hauling. And you would just continue to pay them as if they spent those days working on the ranch. Why not? Who wouldn't love a chance to take a little trip and still get paid for it?"

"Well, I—"

But Loren interrupted. "It'll save these three women considerable money for movers, Reid. When we get home, let's start making plans for this. I can't wait to call Silvie about it! We'll send Raul down in a few days, so we can be at the ranch while he's gone."

"Loren, Loren, is this the same whimpering pussycat who was afraid of a little rain just this morning?" Reid eyed her as if she had changed skins since morning.

"Whimpering pussycat!" Loren exclaimed, grabbing for his nose. "Hey, watch out for that hole! I've never seen a city built around a damned hole!"

He avoided her teasing hands and quipped, "My God! You're not a kitty at all! More like a fighting tiger!" His long arm encircled her shoulders and pulled her against his chest. "Come here, Woman Who Listens. I'll have to tell Emmaline that you're really Tiger Woman! And when you get a crazy notion in your head, you don't listen to anyone!"

"One thing I'm sure of," she purred against him. "I'm not a mountain goat! No more mountain climbing for me!"

He nuzzled her hair, kissing her forehead. "I like tigers best, anyway."

They took their time on the way home, eating a hamburger in Tombstone, "the town too tough to die." When they drove back to the hacienda in Cañada del Oro, dusk was approaching.

Raul hurried out to meet the truck before Reid had time to switch off the engine. The expression on his face told them that something was wrong. Loren froze inside, fearing the worse.

Reid opened the door and shouted, "Is it Dad, Raul? What's wrong?"

CHAPTER TEN

"Oh, Señor Reid," Raul puffed as he ran toward them. His dark face flushed with exertion *or was it something else?*

"Por Dios, hombre! Speak up!" Reid rasped. Patience was not one of his virtues when he was upset.

"It's not Señor Mecena," Raul explained with effort, and Loren detected barely concealed anger. "It's Lupe! Come along. Come on inside."

"Is she ill? What is it?" Reid jerked the truck into park and followed Raul's pace.

"No. She's . . . she's hurt!"

Visions of everything from snakebite to a broken leg filled Loren's mind as she dashed behind the two men. When they entered the kitchen Lupe was sitting at the table, dabbing her eyes with a white handkerchief. She appeared perfectly normal until she turned to face them.

"Por Dios, Lupe! What happened?" Reid demanded, scrutinizing her face.

Raul hovered, nervously stuffing his hands in his pockets. Against the wall stood a gangly youth of about fourteen, of Mexican descent.

"Lupe, darling! You've been hit!" Loren gasped when she was afforded an inspection of the older woman's features.

Lupe's left eye was swollen almost shut and a huge, ugly

bruise under her eye had already turned various stages of red and purple. There was a slight cut in the corner of her lip, but the blood flow had been curtailed. That she had been abused was an obvious deduction.

In disbelief Reid regarded Loren with a bewildered expression. *Hit? Unbelievable!* His instinct resisted the notion, yet his reason knew! "Is it true, Lupe? Have you been hit?" His lips drew back in fury, for he knew, even before she nodded. "Who did it?" His voice was a steel-edged expulsion.

Lupe's voice was a hoarse whisper. "Geraldo."

"Geraldo?" Reid repeated, casting a questioning look at Raul.

"Her husband," Raul said quietly.

Reid's temper exploded loudly. "How in hell could something like this happen? When? Why did you let that bastard in? How could something like this happen right under our noses?" Reid had turned into a raging bull and shot questions at everyone in the room that only Lupe could answer.

"Take it easy, Reid," Loren admonished quietly, placing a cooling hand on one of his flailing arms. "Let's find out what happened."

"That's what I'm trying to do here! Then I'm gonna go out and kill the bastard! How in hell could a man lay a hand on a woman? On Lupe?" His dark eyes burned with his unrelenting rage.

Loren's tone was quiet, but firm. "Reid, I agree. But just calm down a few minutes." She then turned to Lupe, who was once again sniffling into the handkerchief. "Lupe, please stop your crying just long enough to tell us what happened. Have you put anything on that eye?"

"No." Lupe shook her head miserably.

"Well, then," Loren advised as she walked to the refrigerator, "we'd better get some ice on it before it swells any more. I'll just make a quick ice pack for you now. Then we'll talk about what happened." Loren worked while she talked. She grabbed an empty plastic storage bag, filled it with ice cubes, and wrapped the whole thing in a dishtowel. Lupe sat, benumbed, watching Loren, waiting for the soothing ice pack.

Loren knew the makeshift ice bag was temporary, but it had already served its initial purpose, that of diversion. Even the men stood around watching her work and talk, as if it were the most important activity going on at the moment.

"Here you go, Lupe. This will check the swelling and make it feel better." She placed a comforting hand on Lupe's shoulder and sat beside her. "Now, tell us what happened."

Lupe turned somber eyes to Loren and saw another woman who cared, who understood. Ignoring the gaping men around them, she began to pour out her story. "Roberto, my nephew, was home from school today with a sore throat." She gestured to the youth. "He called me around noon to say that Geraldo was at home, demanding to see me. He said that Geraldo wouldn't go away, even when Roberto told him I wasn't there. That I was at work. It only seemed to make Geraldo madder, and he pounded on the doors and windows and caused such a ruckus that he scared Roberto and the neighbors. When Roberto called me *otra vez,* he was scared. So I said I would go and talk to Geraldo. I thought I could make him leave."

She paused, and Loren encouraged. "You left this hacienda?"

"*Sí.* I told Raul where I was going—"

Raul interjected, "And I wanted to go with her. But she

163

said no. I didn't know things were this bad, or I would have gone anyway!"

"So you went back to your home alone?" Loren began.

Lupe nodded. "There he was, beating on the windows and yelling! I think he had been drinking too much beer. I thought we could talk. But he insisted that he was coming back here to live, and he wanted to see the girls. I told him no! He was in no condition to see the girls. And that's when he . . ." Fresh tears started to flow.

"Where is the son of a bitch? I can't wait to get my hands on him!" Reid started in the direction of the door.

"I'm going with you!" Raul barked.

Immediately Lupe rushed forward, grasping Reid's arms with frantic fingers. "Oh, no, Señor Reid! Please, don't do that! Don't hurt him!"

"What?" Reid asked incredulously. "Just look what he did to you, Lupe! There was no one to stop that! And now, you—"

She shook her head fiercely. "I know it! I don't care! I just don't want you to go!" she sobbed.

"Reid!" Loren's voice was steely. "That won't solve anything."

Reid struggled for control. "All right, we'll call the police and let them take over. We'll have him arrested!"

"The police? Oh, no, Señor Reid! Not the police!" Lupe's voice was a plea as she continued to cry and hold his arms.

"Why not? He hit you, Lupe! He's guilty as hell of assault!"

"No! Please don't call the police! I can't explain. I . . . just couldn't do that! He's still my husband. And the father of my children." Her voice trailed to a sad whisper.

"But, Lupe, I just don't understand . . ." Reid sighed

164

heavily and wrung his hands. It was a gesture of helplessness, anger, and frustration.

"Reid," Loren rendered calmly, "it will do no good to call the police if she won't press charges. The police traditionally do not interfere in family squabbles unless the wife is willing to bring charges against the husband."

"Family squabbles? This is no argument! It was a fight!" Reid turned on Loren, his dark eyes deeply passionate. Here was someone on whom he could vent his anger. "You're the lawyer around here, Loren. You seem to have all the answers! What do you suggest we do? Sit around here on our hands until this fool decides to come back and tear the place apart, and Lupe and her children along the way? Speaking of the children, where are the girls, Lupe?"

"They're safe with my neighbor. She usually keeps them after school and is letting them spend the night with her. Geraldo doesn't know her, so he wouldn't suspect where they are." Her sobbing had subsided somewhat.

"Well, I don't want you going back home tonight! It just isn't safe!" Reid decided.

Loren agreed. "I think that's a wise decision, Lupe. You should stay here with us."

Reid paced the floor, clenching his hands in frustration. He felt stymied into doing nothing for his friend and housekeeper. Helpless! He hated the feeling!

Loren recognized the signs of frustration and defeat among those present. She felt them too. But she had seen too many women in similar situations to force an immediate resolution. Decisions made under such times of stress were usually the wrong ones, and this situation needed careful thought and discussion. It would take time. Lupe would need their patient support, for the decisions would have to be hers.

Reid was particularly lacking in that patience. "I don't

like being a sitting duck. And I don't want Lupe to wait around for Geraldo to return. It's unsafe. I want to do something now! Did you come up with any brilliant solutions, lady lawyer?" His voice was a snarl as he vented his anger on the only one in the room who didn't appear helpless.

Loren smiled tolerantly. "Well, you can do something, Reid. And you too, Raul." She pushed Lupe gently by the shoulders back to her seat at the table and pressed the ice pack into her hands. "Take care of that eye, Lupe, darling. Raul, there are some very valuable Indian items in the truck. Would you please bring them in here? I want to show them to Lupe. And be careful!"

"Sí, señorita." Raul started to move, grateful to have something to do.

"Then, Raul, would you please fix up a bed for Roberto in your cabin? I'm sure he is tired."

"Sí." He motioned to the young man. "Vamos, Roberto."

Loren gave Reid an appreciative smile. "Reid, you will be in charge of dinner. Why don't you go out and buy a bucket of fried chicken? That will be adequate for tonight."

The men began to shuffle around, obeying Loren's tactful demands. Reid grumbled under his breath, but followed her orders. He left as Loren and Lupe were poring over the exquisite Navajo rugs and handpainted pots that they had brought from Emmaline Walker's.

By the time the men returned to gather around the table to eat, Lupe was in a much better state. She even nibbled a little on a chicken leg and talked about calling her girls after dinner.

"Reid, I think it's a very good idea for Lupe to spend the night here at the ranch. In fact, she's going to stay right here at the hacienda in one of the extra bedrooms. I want her close tonight. And I know you do too." Loren smiled generously at Reid. He had to agree with the plan. After all, it was his original idea.

Nodding, he sanctioned the arrangement. "I agree, Loren. We want you to be safe and comfortable here, Lupe."

"I know, Señor Reid," Lupe admitted humbly. "I am so lucky to have you and Señorita Loren, who care so much. *Gracias.*"

"Don't mention it, Lupe. It's the very least we can do. Actually it's not enough for me. I wish—"

Loren placed her hand on his arm. "For tonight, this is enough," she interrupted quietly.

Reid's eyes met hers and he understood. He didn't like it, but he understood. Patience was what her silent pleas requested. "Uh, Lupe, while I was out to pick up the chicken, I stopped by the hospital to check on Dad."

"Oh, yes? How is he?" Lupe's expression changed to concern and interest.

"Well"—Reid chuckled—"when the nurses met me in the hall, I figured something was up. It seems that Dad hadn't taken a nap all day, and had been driving them absolutely crazy! He can be such a jackass, you know! The nurses begged me not to awaken him!"

Lupe smiled at the story. "I know exactly what they mean!"

Everyone laughed at her admission.

Reid then announced more satisfying news. "There's even talk of letting him come home, perhaps by next week!"

The announcement was met with definite joy that overpowered the gloom of Lupe's situation. They all talked about the delight of having the old man home again and what needed to be done before that could happen.

"As long as we're talking about plans and changes, we may as well discuss some of the new ones right now while we're all together," Loren instructed, raising her hands to quiet the happy furor.

"What plans?" Reid looked at her curiously.

"Well, if your dad is coming home soon, he will need quality care. Someone close. Someone like Lupe, who knows his quirks as well as the routine of the ranch."

"We will be hiring a home-care nurse, you know. I don't want Lupe to feel overburdened or be responsible for more than she can handle," Reid assured them.

"Good. But Lupe will still be quite busy with the increased duties. And it would be much easier if she lived here at the ranch, don't you think?" Loren posed the question with her head nodding affirmatively.

"Well, sure, but—"

Loren interrupted. "I have persuaded Lupe to move here to the ranch. At least temporarily. She has agreed that she would like that very much. However, she has three children who depend on her."

Reid picked up the suggestion enthusiastically. "They're no problem at all, Lupe. Bring them along! There's plenty of room for them. In fact, we all would love to have the sounds of kids around the ranch." His warm smile canceled any doubts Lupe was harboring.

"Actually you would all be much safer if you lived here, Lupe," Loren urged. "Reid, isn't there an empty guest house?"

"Oh, hell, yes! You'll be perfectly safe here, Lupe. Everyone at the ranch will be informed, and you can be assured that Geraldo will not be allowed on this property! As for the empty guest house, it's probably a mess. It's been sitting unused for years."

"Why don't we take a look at it tomorrow? Perhaps,

with a little work, we could make it livable," Loren suggested.

He shrugged. "Sure. It may take some remodeling, but we can arrange that. It would be perfect for you, Lupe."

"Great! We'll work on that tomorrow," Loren stated decisively. "Meantime Raul can go down to Bisbee, haul that furniture up to Window Rock, and beat it back here in time to help move Lupe to the hacienda. We need to get settled before your father gets home, Reid. And there's so much to do! What's wrong? Didn't you tell Raul about Emmaline Walker and her daughters?" Loren laughed at the startled expressions around her. She stood and began gathering up the chicken refuse, piling it in the bucket. "Well, Reid, you explain the situation to Raul, and I'm sure he'll be more than happy to help them. They need your help so badly, Raul." She smiled reassuringly at the dark-skinned man, who didn't dare question her.

Reid watched with amusement as she bustled around the kitchen. They all nodded in agreement because there was no opposing Loren's rationale. It was too reasonable. The solution for Lupe made sense. And the plan for the Navajo women only needed to be expedited. With a chuckle Reid spread his hands. "Well, I asked for brilliant solutions from our lady lawyer. Looks like we have them! And our work cut out for us!"

"I'm glad you agree. Now, I'm going to see that Lupe gets a good hot bath, and a safe bed for the night." She draped her arm around the older woman's shoulders and led her down the hall.

"Oh, no, Señorita Loren. You don't have to—" Lupe protested.

However, she met with the same obstinacy that the men had. "Nonsense, Lupe. You took care of me last night, didn't you? Tonight it's my turn. It's only fair. This is something I want to do. A hot bath will make you feel so much better." Their voices dwindled down the hall and the two men and young boy looked at each other for a moment. Then Reid followed orders and proceeded to explain to Raul about Emmaline Walker and the family of women who needed him.

Later, as Loren rummaged through the hall closet for another blanket for Lupe, Reid stepped outside his guest bedroom. "Loren, how's Lupe?"

"She's a little chilled. I think it's probably shock after such a traumatic day. This has been quite an unpleasant, frightening experience for her."

"For all of us. Uh, I want to apologize for the way I talked to you earlier in the evening, Loren. I was just so upset, I couldn't think straight. I know I was too harsh with you, and I don't even know why."

"Don't worry about it, Reid. I understand." She smiled in the dark.

His hand reached for her arm. "Hey, hey, lady lawyer, when you get rolling, you really churn! You know just what to say when everyone else is hysterical. I'll admit you handled us all very well. Especially Lupe."

"Thank you, Reid. I've seen these cases before, unfortunately."

"Have you seen this before?" He pulled her against him, kissing her thoroughly.

"Yes," she whispered. "But I'm not sure how to handle it."

"I have some suggestions. You're invited into my guest room, unless, of course, I'm invited back into my own bedroom."

She gazed into his darkly passionate eyes and shook her head. "Not tonight, Reid. Lupe may need me."

"Lupe? What about me?"

"Lupe's been through a disturbing experience today. Surely you understand."

"So have I. I've seen my lady lawyer in action, and I'm still reeling! Whatever happened to the young girl I carried up to that antique brass bed on Prince Street?"

Loren rose to tiptoe and kissed his lips quickly. "She grew up. Did I thank you for taking me to Bisbee? It was a lovely day, Reid."

"When are you going to thank me properly?"

With a mysterious smile she disappeared behind Lupe's door, hugging the blanket and thinking of Reid's warm body that she was refusing.

The last few days in Arizona were a whirlwind of activity. Loren assumed direction of the varied activities while Reid assisted and watched her in amazement. What else could he do? She was damned right and damned efficient. God! She was remarkable!

By the time they left, Lupe was in tears, and Raul puffed up like a frog. His smile was tight. Even the aging Senator Mecena, who had only been with her for a few days, was sad to see the whirlwind of energy, this Loren of Reid's past, take off over the saguaro shadows. Everyone feared the same thing . . . that they would never see her again. So did Reid.

CHAPTER ELEVEN

"You're right, Loren," Reid admitted as he reached for his gin and tonic. "There is nothing quite like this in Tucson. There is a feeling here, an electricity in the air, that's hard to explain."

The waitress, elegantly gowned in black, flowed away from them. Her dress swayed to the jazz beat from the grand piano. The Jockey Club. Cosmopolitan. Plush. Elite. Polished wood and oriental style. Sophisticated.

"Of course, Tucson has its own special beauty, Reid. The Westward Look was lovely, overlooking the city. And the view from your veranda when the sun sets behind the Tucson Mountains is absolutely unsurpassed." Loren's face lit up with pleasure. She was in her element, and Reid knew it. She looked so much a natural part of the sophistication of the place—oriental rugs, overstuffed chairs, jazz tinkling from the ivory keys of a distant piano . . . and Loren. Beautiful Loren, with her bluebonnet-colored eyes, her tawny hair falling softly to her shoulders, her slender figure embellished by the folds of a silky, cream-colored gown with a daring slit that revealed a portion of gorgeous leg. God! How he loved her! How he wanted her!

"All that can be yours, Loren," he offered seriously.

She sipped her drink with style. "I feel very lucky to have had a chance to visit Arizona. I received a call today

172

from Silvie Tanner in Window Rock. The check came last week along with a letter of apology from the State Department and a merit of commendation for PFC Benjamin Walker from the Marines." Loren smiled warmly. "She says that Emmaline values the letters more than the Silver Star!"

"She would." Reid nodded with a smile.

"Apparently everyone is settled and happy in their new home. She and Emmaline are weaving and making pots like crazy in preparation for the spring and summer tourist seasons next year. And Tracy and the baby are happily reunited with Paul." There was a glow of satisfaction and pride on her face.

"So everyone is living happily ever after," Reid muttered, sounding more bitter than he had intended. He didn't begrudge these most deserving of people some bit of happiness in their lives. All he wanted in the world was her!

Loren flashed instantly. "They are living in harmony with themselves and what they want to do with their lives. That's most important to me."

His hand covered hers affectionately. "You're right, Loren. I know that you made a large contribution to that happiness they are now experiencing. I'm proud of you. In the same way, the people in my household owe you a debt of gratitude. For such a goddamn mess, you left things running pretty smoothly at the hacienda. Dad is extremely happy to have Lupe so close. And now that she's had time to think, she has decided to file for divorce. I'm relieved just to know that she and her family are living at Casa del Oro. They're safe. The kids are having a ball! Roberto is working with Raul on the ranch after school and making a little money. Lupe's girls get to swim daily in the pool, and are very happy with their new living quarters."

"Wonderful. You did say you wanted children running all over the ranch, didn't you, Reid?" Loren reminded him with a grin.

His dark eyes reflected something deeper. "I meant my own children, not Lupe's."

Loren chose not to pursue his statement. "How is Lupe?"

"Her face has almost healed, and she is doing fine. You were right to leave her be—another brilliant solution by my lady lawyer. I'll admit it; I was ready to tear the bastard limb from limb when I found that he had hit her! I don't remember when I've ever been so angry!"

Loren nodded, recalling the chaos of that night. "I know. But it wouldn't have solved anything to have you in jail for assault."

"Perhaps it wouldn't have helped Lupe," he acknowledged. "But, it would have made me feel a hell of a lot better!"

"There are other, better ways, to deal with your aggression, Reid." Loren smiled seductively.

His finger made slow circles along her wrist. "Would you help me deal with my aggression, lady lawyer?"

"Later." She chuckled low. "Right now I would like to have dinner. I'm starved! I was so busy today, I skipped lunch altogether."

"You work too hard," he assessed seriously.

"There's so much to do."

"You can't do it all, Loren. Can't solve everyone's problems."

"I know." She smiled wistfully, thinking that she couldn't even solve her own. "Tonight is just beautiful, Reid. I enjoy this relaxing atmosphere so much, I could sit here all night and listen to that gorgeous man in the corner make love to that piano! Have you ever heard such

174

fantastic jazz renditions?" Loren's eyes were dreamy as she swayed to a few bars of the song.

Reid pulled her to her feet. "I would rather make love to you."

"Dinner first," she teased.

"Promise? Or do I have to worry about running into Mark? I have horrible visions of someday hiding in your closet, boots in hand, in very embarrassing attire."

Loren laughed at the mental picture he painted. "Don't worry. There's not a chance! My relationship with Mark is definitely over. He was none too happy with my trip to Arizona."

They were escorted to a cozy corner, where they resumed the conversation privately. Loren requested oysters Rockefeller. Reid ordered steak, rare.

"So Mark was displeased with the fact that you spent a week with me in Arizona?" Reid quipped. "I can't imagine why that would upset him."

"I returned the engagement ring." The visible symbol of another man in her life was gone. Now, again, it was just the two of them.

Reid's hand covered hers in a reflexive gesture. His dark eyes explored her face. "How do you feel about it?"

"Relieved." She smiled faintly.

"Me too." His fingertips caressed the place where the ring had been. It was as if that was one place on her body that he had never touched, and he had to make sure it was free. "What was Mark's reaction?"

"Actually I think he expected it. Ours wasn't an intimate association. He raised hell because I failed to take care of business."

"What business?"

"He gave me a couple of names of people connected with his copper mine. I was to look them up while I was

175

in Tucson. He wanted me to visit the mine and personally see how things were going. Honestly, Reid, I forgot all about it. I tried to tell him about how busy I was with Lupe and your father and the Navajo women, but he wouldn't listen. He didn't feel that they were important. The mine, and whatever money he's making or losing on the damn thing, are foremost to him."

Reid shook his head. "I must say, Loren, Mark has been a wealth of information for me. His connections have been invaluable. He has pushed this water bill. In fact, he's partly responsible for my opportunity tomorrow to testify before the Interior Committee. Plus, it was his idea to change our tactics."

"How's that?" Loren couldn't believe that Mark had been so helpful to Reid. Actually, though, she shouldn't be surprised. He had his reasons.

"Well, we've divided up the various aspects that were included in the original bill. We're going after each problem separately, instead of tacking on additional requests that the committee may feel will cost much in federal funds. The other way gives them any number of reasons to vote it down. Now they can consider each bill, with its specific legislation, separately."

"And that was Mark's idea?"

"Yes, and it only makes sense. You see, when the bill was first drafted we added a few extra items that we knew would be good for the state. I mean, we figured to take advantage when we had the chance. Mark pointed out the fallacy in that thinking, at least in these tight economic times."

"So you're making a presentation to the Interior Committee tomorrow?"

"I'll be presenting my case in the morning and fielding questions along with the governor in the afternoon. After

176

that . . ." He shrugged, and they both knew what was after that. *He would be leaving Washington.*

Loren didn't want to think of it. She smiled a false smile as the elegantly attired waiter brought their dinner. They were together on borrowed time, and they both knew it. They would be forced apart again. And soon!

The next day Loren came home from work early, after meeting with a client near Alexandria. She had been extremely nervous and edgy in the few weeks since returning from Arizona. Even Althea, her partner, commented that she hadn't returned from the trip rested at all. But Loren knew what was gnawing at her insides, waking her up at dawn, plaguing her every time she looked at Reid. Just as she walked in the door, the phone rang.

"Hello?" Her tone was tired.

Loren was instantly alert as an anxious voice with a Mexican accent related events at Casa del Oro. The most feared, the worst, the dreaded inevitable—they had all known it would happen. But now? So soon? Why, oh, why? The age-old questions that accompany sorrow surged forth.

"Oh, Lupe, noooo." She sank into her chair. She listened and advised Lupe to be strong, that Reid needed her to be. Yes, she would get in touch with Reid as soon as possible. When she cradled the phone, Loren buried her face in her hands. There were no tears, but she was grieving just the same. They were losing the senator . . . and she was losing Reid. Loren was doubly grieved.

Hours later, his knock was hard and sharp. Almost before he let himself in the door, Loren had wrapped herself around him, her arms encircling his waist, her heart pressed fervently to his.

"Hey! Is this all I get for congratulations? The hearing

was very positive! Have you seen the news yet? The bill is a shoe-in with all the backers we need. Come on, Loren. You need to change. We're meeting the governor in an hour for dinner!"

"Oh, Reid." She buried the words against him, not caring about anything at the moment but him.

"Loren?" His large hands grasped her shoulders and tried to pry her from the tight clasp. "Hey, baby, what's wrong?" One hand slid around taut shoulders and under her hair.

"Reid, Reid, it's your father. . . ."

He froze.

She knew she had to tell him. With effort she forced herself to look at him. His chin was squared, as if waiting for her to hit him. In effect, he was. His lips, usually so soft and willing, were tight and framed austerely across the top by his dark mustache. His dark eyes, deep and unflinching, examined her as he waited for what she had to say. *Oh, God, how could she let him go?*

"I—I got a call from Lupe. She was nearly hysterical. Your father suffered another stroke four hours ago and was taken by ambulance to the hospital. Raul and the nurse are there with him. They think he is dying. Oh, Reid, I'm so sorry." She cupped his drawn face with her hands and kissed him. Then they embraced for long, agonizing moments.

With a heavy sigh he shifted, moving stiffly away from her. "I, uh, I'll call the hospital and talk to the nurse first. Then I'll decide what to do." He shrugged out of his dark suit coat as he reached for the phone. Fifteen minutes later he turned to Loren. "He has suffered severe damage and probably won't make it through the night. I have to go soon."

"I know. Would you like a cup of coffee?"

"Yes." He ran his hand over his face, as if to clear his thinking. It had been a busy, high-level day. He had looked forward to relaxing tonight with Loren. But it wasn't to be. Not tonight. . . .

They sat together at the small table that overlooked the tiny, formal garden outside her window.

"Loren, will you go back with me?"

Her voice was strained. "Certainly, Reid. If you want me to."

He rose and paced the floor impatiently. "I don't want you to go along just to wait at the hospital until my father dies. I want you to go with me to Arizona—to marry me."

How . . . why . . . could he think of marriage at a time like this?

"Reid, please don't press for that decision at this time." She sounded remarkably calm. Inside she was screaming.

"This is not a sudden decision. The question was asked six years ago. That should have given you enough time to weigh your decision."

"Reid, you can't go back that far."

"Why not?" There was a hardness, a firmness, about his tone, his face, his entire body. "I loved you then. And I love you now, more deeply than ever. I want you, Loren. I want you to be my wife. Now."

The tension in the air was so strong, Loren could almost reach out and touch it. All that they had been through and all that they meant to each other was suddenly on trial. Their future was at stake. For months now, years actually, they had skirted the issue, avoided mentioning the ultimate. Now they were on the brink of another abyss in their lives. Would they plunge into the darkness again?

"Reid, I love you too. You know that." Her voice was strained and Loren stopped to swallow. "But I just don't see how—"

"Wait!" He was pacing, gesturing his frustration. "Am I going crazy? We've got two people here who love each other and yet you're saying you don't see how we can work this out?"

"No, that wasn't what I was about to say," she answered quietly. "I don't see how you can ask me to give up everything I've worked for all these years. My career, my personal goals, my home. It isn't fair to me."

"Fair?" he barked. "Love isn't fair? Marriage isn't the answer? Most women want it. What's wrong with you, Loren?"

Loren wanted to say yes, unconditionally. However, something beyond her control restrained her, reminded her that she must be true to herself as well. That there was another way. Yet a niggling thought in the back of her mind questioned it still. She sighed and cleared her throat. "I—I've given this a lot of thought, Reid. There is another solution."

He stopped pacing and narrowed his dark eyes at her. "Well, I'm glad to know you've considered the fact that I love you. And the likelihood that I would ask you to marry me . . . again! So what is my brilliant lady lawyer's decision this time?"

Was it sarcasm or sheer male frustration that permeated his tones?

"I—I will always love you, Reid, and be here for you." She couldn't meet his black gaze when she said it.

"Here? In D.C.? Then you're refusing me again?"

There was an uncomfortable pause. "No. I'm not denying our love at all, Reid. I'm admitting it. I cherish it . . . and you. And I will always be yours. I will be your . . . mistress." She couldn't believe she was actually saying it, that she was considering such a life for herself. For

180

them. It went against everything she stood for, and yet it seemed to her the only way.

His staccato words jerked her eyes up to him. "My mistress? Loren? Are you serious? Is this what you really want for us?"

"No," she whispered hoarsely. "But it's the only solution I could figure. I just can't pick up and leave. Neither can you!"

"Only solution? My God, woman! I'm offering you my love, marriage, my ranch, everything I own and value in the world! Why do you insist on throwing our love away again?"

"I'm not throwing it away. I will save it for you, and only you, Reid. Don't you understand? I will be yours alone."

"Here. In Washington." His tone was flat and empty. "Yes."

He strode away from her, pacing the small kitchen like a caged lion, his rage on the brink. Suddenly his fury exploded in a blaze of energy. "I don't want a mistress, Loren! I want you as my wife! In Arizona! With kids running all over the ranch! Our kids! Is that so impossible to ask?"

"How can you ask me to give up all I've worked for these past six years?" She stood and met his fury steadily. It was something she believed in and she had to defend it. She had given up six agonizing years of his love for this. It had to be a strong conviction. And she had to convince him of its importance to her. She couldn't make him understand before. Now her position was even stronger. She had more at stake.

"I'm not asking you to give up a thing, Loren! I'm asking you to be my wife! There are no strings attached to that."

181

"I—I can't." Her voice was weak. Would he ever understand?

"Why? Why the hell not?" His dark eyes settled on her sadly and his voice was a hoarse whisper. He was losing again, and he wasn't sure why.

Loren took a deep breath. "I was only thirteen when my mother died. It's a very impressionable age, and I remember her well. She was an unhappy woman here in Washington with my father and me."

"Loren, *querida,* I'm sorry about that part of your life. But what does that have to do with us?"

"Oh, God, Reid, please try to understand what I'm about to say. From a woman's view . . . from *my* view!" Her blue eyes begged, and he nodded his willingness. How could he do otherwise?

Loren slumped at the small table and continued to talk. "When my mother married Dad, she gave up a promising career in the theater. She wasn't able to pursue her personal goals here in Washington. As a politician's wife, she was involved in a social whirl beyond her control. You know what it's like. There was always something going on. She felt totally unfulfilled and blamed it on my father, especially after she became ill. I watched her bitterness grow. We don't want that to happen to our relationship, Reid." Tears filled her blue eyes as Loren implored him to understand. "I vowed that I would not compromise my goals for a man. Six years ago I felt the same way, but my career wasn't as satisfying then as it is now. I love my job and can't give it up. I will not jeopardize our relationship with the bitterness that comes from self-sacrifice."

Reid's reaction was not at all what she expected. No more angry outbursts. No pacing and raving. He sat down opposite her, encasing her icy hands in his warm, capable ones, and smiled. A gentle smile that revealed the single dimple in one cheek that she loved so much. In a low tone he asked, "Is that why, Loren? Is that why you refused me six years ago? Were you afraid of losing your identity and goals, for me?"

She nodded sadly but gratefully, her heart reaching out to the man she loved. He understood! What had seemed like an insurmountable explanation was summed up by Reid in a few succinct words . . . and with a smile. Her career was important to her, and she didn't want him to belittle it as Mark had done.

"Do you want to have your career and a family too? Or are you saying that you don't desire the same things I do?"

One nervous hand reached to caress his face. "Oh, Reid, I love you so. I do want you. And a family. I still grieve that I lost our baby six years ago. But—"

"Well, then, my lovely lady lawyer, surely you can figure out how to juggle all of that. I have never—*never* —asked you to give up anything in order to marry me! I wouldn't make demands like that on you, Loren, especially since it's so vital to you. All I'm asking is that you be my wife. You don't have to give up your career."

"But, Arizona is where you live—"

"For now it is, *querida*. You can keep your clients here in D.C. and set up an office there too. *Dios mío!* Look what you did for the few women you met in Arizona, and you were only there a week! Imagine what you could do if you lived there! They need you. And so do I, *mi amor.*" As if to convince her, Reid moved deftly to her side, urging her up into his strong arms. Large hands gently cupped her face, turning it to meet his ardent lips. The kiss conveyed a love that had endured six long, lonely years and convinced her that a future together was possible. *Possible!*

"Two offices?" she murmured, when he lifted his lips. "Are you sure I . . . we can manage that?"

He kissed her again, little sipping kisses, as though he were tasting fine wine all over her face. "Of course! I'll fly you across the country to keep up with your eastern clients. People do it all the time. I don't think I could stop you, Loren, but after seeing you in action, I wouldn't want to. Your job is valuable, to others as well as to you. This is something you should do. We can make it work. We will, *mi amor.*"

"Then we'll keep this little town house?"

He kissed a sizzling trail to her earlobe. "Sure. Who knows? I may consider a political career in the future. I've grown to love this city, too, especially if I can be here with you. When we come back for business, we'll need a place to stay."

"I—I just didn't think of being in both places." She smiled with relief, stretching eager arms around his neck.

Reid's capable hands were stroking her back, positioning her against him. "You didn't ask your man, lady lawyer. You should have known I would figure out a way to keep you this time. I couldn't let you go . . . couldn't leave you. Loren, I have always loved you. From the moment I first saw you, first made love to you in that antique brass bed upstairs, I fell in love with the lady with the bluest eyes I've ever seen."

She pulled his lips down to hers. "And I fell in love with the dark-eyed cowboy with scuffy boots from Arizona."

His kiss halted her words and caught her breath. "That sea captain's wife and her Hessian lover had nothing on us, *mi amor.*"

Loren giggled as a light giddiness overwhelmed her. She had wasted so much time worrying, wondering, mourning Reid's loss, even before he was gone, that she just couldn't shift her thinking so quickly. All she knew was that she wouldn't be losing him. They would be together, and she wouldn't be losing anything. She would be gaining everything!

"Reid." She approached him seriously. "Do you really think it will work? I can keep my office here? My clients? Our town house? And have children running over the ranch?"

He shrugged. "We can handle all of that. The kids are up to you, Loren. Can we have another child?"

"Sure. The doctor told me there was no reason why I couldn't. Well, only one reason . . ." She hedged with a teasing twinkle in her eye.

"I'll certainly do my part!" Reid assured her heartily with a grin. "You can have it all, *mi amor.* Anything you want." His kisses reached the pulsing hollow of her throat, then blazed a lower trail.

Loren arched her breasts against his hot lips. "Anything?"

"Hmmm. But not now. Although I want like hell to carry you upstairs to that little brass bed right now, I do have to leave for Arizona."

"I'll go with you, Reid. I want to be there. So we both have things to do and phone calls to make." Loren was suddenly serious.

"I'll cancel dinner with the governor and make reservations on the first flight out."

"Reservations? We're not flying in your plane?"

"There isn't time. We'll fly back later to get it. It'll give us a good excuse to make love again in the brass bed!"

Loren smiled, her blue eyes glistening with happiness. "I'll call Althea and tell her the good news."

Burying warm kisses between her breasts, he murmured, "Break it to her gently."

"Yes, gently . . ." Loren felt a great surge of joy rising within her.

"And don't forget next spring."

"Next spring?"

Reid's mouth was muffled against her heated breasts. "In the bluebonnets . . . in Texas . . . you and me . . ."

Loren's laughter echoed against ancient brick walls and floated up narrow stairs past the brass bed, through the attic of the little town house on Prince Street.

LOOK FOR NEXT MONTH'S
CANDLELIGHT ECSTASY ROMANCES®

When You Want A Little More Than Romance—

Try A Candlelight Ecstasy!

SWEET WILD WIND

by Joyce Verrette

In the primeval forests of America, passion was born in the mystery of a stolen kiss.

A high-spirited beauty, daughter of the furrier to the French king, Aimee Dessaline had led a sheltered life. But on one fateful afternoon, her fate was sealed with a burning kiss. Vale's sun bronzed skin and buckskins proclaimed his Indian upbringing, but his words belied another heritage. Convinced that he was a spy, she vowed to forget him—this man they called Valjean d'Auvergne, Comte de la Tour.

But not even the glittering court at Versailles where Parisian royalty courted her favors, not even the perils of the war torn wilderness could still her impetuous heart.

A DELL BOOK   17634-4   ($3.95)

Seize The Dawn

by Vanessa Royall

For as long as she could remember, Elizabeth Rolfson knew that her destiny lay in America. She arrived in Chicago in 1885, the stunning heiress to a vast empire. As men of daring pressed westward, vying for the land, Elizabeth was swept into the savage struggle. Driven to learn the secret of her past, to find the one man who could still the restlessness of her heart, she would stand alone against the mighty to claim her proud birthright and grasp a dream of undying love.

A DELL BOOK   17788-X $3.50

Desert Hostage

Diane Dunaway

Behind her is England and her first innocent encounter with love. Before her is a mysterious land of forbidding majesty. Kidnapped, swept across the deserts of Araby, Juliette Barclay sees her past vanish in the endless, shifting sands. Desperate and defiant, she seeks escape only to find harrowing danger, to discover her one hope in the arms of her captor, the Shiek of El Abadan. Fearless and proud, he alone can tame her. She alone can possess his soul. Between them lies the secret that will bind her to him forever, a woman possessed, a slave of love.

A DELL BOOK   11963-4   **$3.95**

NEW DELL

CANDLELIGHT Ecstasy Supreme

LOVERS AND PRETENDERS,
by Prudence Martin
$2.50

Christine and Paul—looking for new lives on a cross-country jaunt, were bound by lies and a passion that grew more dangerously honest with each passing day. Would the truth destroy their love?

WARMED BY THE FIRE,
by Donna Kimel Vitek
$2.50

When malicious gossip forces Juliet to switch jobs from one television network to another, she swears an office romance will never threaten her career again—until she meets superstar anchorman Marc Tyner.